DANIEL X

LIGHTS OUT

Books by James Patterson
for Young Readers

The Daniel X Novels
The Dangerous Days of Daniel X (with Michael Ledwidge)
Watch the Skies (with Ned Rust)
Demons and Druids (with Adam Sadler)
Game Over (with Ned Rust)
Armageddon (with Chris Grabenstein)
Lights Out (with Chris Grabenstein)

The Middle School Novels
Middle School, The Worst Years of My Life
(with Chris Tebbetts, illustrated by Laura Park)
Middle School: Get Me out of Here!
(with Chris Tebbetts, illustrated by Laura Park)
Middle School: Big Fat Liar
(with Lisa Papademetriou, illustrated by Neil Swaab)
Middle School: How I Survived Bullies, Broccoli, and Snake Hill
(with Chris Tebbetts, illustrated by Laura Park)
Middle School: Ultimate Showdown
(with Julia Bergen, illustrated by Alec Longstreth)
Middle School: Save Rafe!
(with Chris Tebbetts, illustrated by Laura Park)
Middle School: Just My Rotten Luck
(with Chris Tebbetts, illustrated by Laura Park)

The I Funny Novels
I Funny (with Chris Grabenstein, illustrated by Laura Park)
I Even Funnier (with Chris Grabenstein, illustrated by Laura Park)
I Totally Funniest (with Chris Grabenstein, illustrated by Laura Park)

The Treasure Hunters Novels
Treasure Hunters
(with Chris Grabenstein and Mark Shulman, illustrated by Juliana Neufeld)
Treasure Hunters: Danger Down the Nile
(with Chris Grabenstein, illustrated by Juliana Neufeld)

Other Illustrated Novels
House of Robots (with Chris Grabenstein, illustrated by Juliana Neufeld)
Public School Superhero (with Chris Tebbetts, illustrated by Cory Thomas)
Daniel X: Alien Hunter (graphic novel; with Leopoldo Gout)
Daniel X: The Manga, Vols. 1–3 (with SeungHui Kye)

For previews of upcoming books in these series and other information, visit
middleschoolbooks.com, ifunnybooks.com, and treasurehuntersbooks.com.

For more information about the author, visit JamesPatterson.com.

DANIEL X

LIGHTS OUT

JAMES PATTERSON
AND CHRIS GRABENSTEIN

LITTLE, BROWN AND COMPANY
New York Boston

Copyright © 2015 by James Patterson
Daniel X® is a trademark of JBP Business, LLC.

Little, Brown and Company

Hachette Book Group
1290 Avenue of the Americas, New York, NY 10104
Visit us at lb-kids.com

Little, Brown and Company is a division of Hachette Book Group, Inc.
The Little, Brown name and logo are trademarks of Hachette Book Group, Inc.

The publisher is not responsible for websites (or their content) that are not owned by the publisher.

First Edition: July 2015

Library of Congress Cataloging-in-Publication Data

Patterson, James, 1947–
Lights out / James Patterson and Chris Grabenstein. — First edition.
    pages cm. — (Daniel X ; [6])
Summary: "Daniel X is finally ready to take on the universe's most evil alien outlaw that killed his parents years ago, but he will need all his friends—and superpowers—to make it out alive"— Provided by publisher.
    ISBN 978-0-316-20745-4 (hc) — ISBN 978-0-316-40461-7 (large print) — ISBN 978-0-316-20746-1 (ebook) [1. Extraterrestrial beings—Fiction. 2. Friendship—Fiction. 3. Orphans—Fiction. 4. Science fiction.] I. Grabenstein, Chris. II. Title.
    PZ7.P27653Lig 2015
    [Fic]—dc23

                                                        2014032553

10 9 8 7 6 5 4 3 2 1

RRD-C

Printed in the United States of America

PROLOGUE

One

IT SHOULD'VE BEEN a perfect night.

I was out for a midnight stroll along a dark, deserted highway, somewhere in the middle of Kentucky. Billions of stars were scattered across the sky like sparkling diamonds on black velvet. The air was so crisp and clear I could see the Milky Way. I could also pinpoint several of the planets I've visited during my dangerous days on Earth as the Alien Hunter. It's true. I may only be a teenager, but I've racked up some serious intergalactic frequent flyer miles working my way through the list of Alien Outlaws on Terra Firma.

Quick CliffsNotes: Terra Firma is what we friendly neighborhood extraterrestrials call your planet. The alien outlaws who are here to destroy it? They basically call you guys "dead meat."

Anyway, I had recently taken out Number 2, the second-most heinous, foul, and all-around evil creature on The List, so I should've been feeling pretty good, right?

You'd think I'd take a victory orbit around your planet or dump a cooler of ice water over my head, the way athletes do when they win the Super Bowl or the World Series.

There was only one problem: After you take down Number 2, guess who's left?

You nailed it: *Number 1.*

Everything I had ever done in my life had been leading up to my next and most powerful enemy.

It was finally time to take down the top dog. I needed to eliminate, once and for all, the abominable alien who looked like a slimy, NBA-sized praying mantis (which is how he earned his nickname, The Prayer). If you're wondering how this overgrown, bug-ugly insect became Number 1 on my hit list, the answer's easy: he was the ruthless monster who brutally murdered my mother and father twelve years ago back in Kansas. I was three at the time, but trust me, I remember each and every gory detail.

So, as I was walking along that peaceful highway in the middle of the night, a certain '80s hair-band tune was blaring through my head: "The Final Countdown." That's the 1986 rock anthem with the synthesized keyboard riff that gets blasted through stadium speakers right before the biggest sports games of the season.

Because this was it. My last round in the ring. My NCAA finals. My *sudden-death overtime.* The big test all the little tests had been leading up to.

So I wasn't just out for a starlit stroll, even though the night sky was full of hope and promise and wondrous far-off worlds. I was out there racking my alien brain, trying to formulate some sort of plan to take down Number 1—a plan that didn't include me *dying*.

The way my parents did when they went up against the six-and-a-half-foot-tall insectoid with the bulging, plum-colored body and stringy red dreadlocks dangling down between his antennae.

Oh, yeah. Number 1 is a real charmer.

Suddenly an air horn blared behind me.

I whipped around.

A speeding tractor trailer came roaring up the road out of nowhere.

I did the math. Analyzed the trajectory.

The answer wasn't good: the 18-wheeler would be plowing into me in the blink of an eye.

Two

IN THE NANOSECOND before I joined the bugs splattered all over the big rig's engine grille, I tried to stop the truck by using my imagination.

That's right. My imagination.

I was born with the strange ability to rearrange material at will. And being able to create whatever I need, whenever I need it, is a superpower way better than shooting sticky spider webs out of your wrists, beaming infrared rays from your eyeballs, bending your rubbery body, or flying faster than a speeding bullet. Hey, if I want to do *any* of those things (and a billion others) all I have to do is imagine myself doing them.

You might have trouble buying into what I'm talking about. The power to create and manipulate the atomic structure of objects around me (including a mammoth Mack truck) is completely, well, *alien* to you earthlings. But it's just part of who I am. Kind of like having blue eyes. Only much more useful.

Anyway, in the split second before being splattered, I decided to put a ten-foot-thick steel wall between me and the monster truck.

I'd also make sure the truck driver was buckled in tight and that he had deployable air bags. Hey, I didn't want either one of us ending up as tomorrow's blue plate special at The Roadkill Café.

I concentrated on the image of the steel barricade, *hard*. I have to be totally focused on what I'm creating to pull off even a simple transformation like this one. But in terms of difficulty, blocking oncoming traffic with an impenetrable wall is the kind of atom scrambling I can usually do with both hands tied behind my back.

Usually.

But not that night.

The truck slammed into me. Sent me flying.

There was no ten-foot-thick steel wall. Just ten tons of pain and agony.

I hit the asphalt. Then double sets of steel-belted radials crunched across my legs. I heard my ribs splinter and my finger bones snap.

I have never felt such excruciating pain.

Never.

Not even when the late Number 2 turned me into a tumbling boulder and sent me rolling down the jagged side of a molten mountain.

Something had gone horribly wrong. My creative powers? My amazing imagination? They'd failed me. Big time.

As I lay moaning on the pavement, slipping in and out

of consciousness, I remember thinking, "How did this happen? How *could* this happen?"

I had been fully focused. I was totally rested. My powers were completely charged and ready to rock.

But I couldn't even conjure up a simple wall?

How could it happen?

And then I heard a terrifying voice screeching inside my head.

A voice I remembered from when I was three years old, hiding behind an old water heater in the basement of my Kansas home.

How do you think it happened, Danny Boy?

It was him.

It was Number 1.

The Prayer.

PART ONE
GETTING TO NUMBER 1

Chapter 1

WHEN I FINALLY woke up, I was in a strange and sterile place.

A hospital. More specifically, a hospital bed.

I creaked open my aching eyes (yes, even my eyelids hurt) and saw an IV pole with drip bags hanging off it. Some kind of pump with a glowing LED readout was clamped to its side. Behind the pole, on a rolling cart, a blipping screen charted the rhythm of my heartbeat.

My bed had guardrails and buttons for moving the mattress up and down—just like in those Craftmatic Adjustable Bed commercials I've seen on late night TV when I'm checking out the Syfy channel to see if they've gotten things right.

"Well, look who's awake," said a soft voice above me.

I craned my head to the right and saw a nurse dressed in scrubs with a stethoscope draped around her neck. I tried to activate my zoom vision to read the nametag pinned to her chest (usually my eyes can do a 128:1 telephoto push), but all I got for my efforts was a dull, throbbing headache and some blurred double vision.

"I'm Nurse O'Hara," she said with a smile. "It's so good to see your beautiful blue eyes, Daniel."

"Where am I?"

"The hospital. Intensive care."

I tried to sit up.

"Now, now," said Nurse O'Hara as she gently eased me back down into the bed. "You mustn't push yourself, Danny Boy."

"What?"

"I said, you mustn't push yourself…"

"No. What did you call me?"

"Danny Boy."

I remembered hearing Number 1 call me Danny Boy. In my head. Right after that Mack truck plowed over me with nine of its eighteen wheels.

Nurse O'Hara's smile broadened. "Forgive me, Daniel. I'm very Irish." She bent down and gave me a sweet hug. "Saints be praised! You're alive!"

Three doctors (well, three people in white lab coats with their names embroidered over the breast pockets) stepped into the room.

"Good morning, Daniel. We heard the good news," said one who looked like Dr. Sanjay Gupta, the chief medical correspondent on CNN. Only this Dr. Gupta had an even brighter, wider smile.

"It's a miracle," said Nurse O'Hara, wiping a tear from her rosy cheek.

"Indeed," said another one of the doctors, who looked like the extremely happy cousin of that other TV doctor, Dr. Oz.

"Definitely," added the third doctor with a toothy smile. She reminded me of the lady on *Grey's Anatomy*.

Okay, I watch a lot of doctor shows on TV. Human anatomy fascinates me. (You guys have screwy plumbing.) Besides, my alien brain operates like an iPod with unlimited free downloads. But right then, I didn't have time for smiley doctors. I needed to drag my butt out of bed and go hunt down Number 1.

"Thanks for the hospitality, guys," I said. "But I need to hit the road."

I went to tug the IV needle out of my arm. Four pairs of hands restrained me.

"No, Daniel," said the Dr. Oz look-alike. "You need to rest."

"I can't. I have a job to do."

"Your only job, young man," said Nurse O'Hara, "is to get better. You were in a horrible accident."

I laughed a little. "Yeah. That happens to me a lot."

"This is no laughing matter, Daniel," said the female doctor. "You've been in a very deep coma."

Okay. Ms. Grey's Anatomy had my attention. "A coma? For how long?"

She glanced at the one I called Dr. Oz. He nodded his head, giving her permission to tell me the awful truth.

"Over a year, Daniel. You have been unconscious for thirteen months."

Chapter 2

"THIRTEEN MONTHS?" I blurted. "That's impossible."

The doctors shook their heads.

"We've spent a lot of time together, Danny Boy," said Nurse O'Hara. "I strung twinkling lights in the window and hung ornaments off your IV pole, hoping the visual stimulation might..."

"No," I said, sitting up in my bed. "This is crazy...."

I saw Dr. Oz bury his hand into the hip pocket of his lab coat and fiddle with something. None of the doctors were smiling anymore.

"Look, I appreciate everything you've done for me. But if I've been stuck in here for thirteen months because of that little fender bender out on the highway, that means I'm way behind schedule."

Okay. I was starting to panic. Supercharged adrena-line was pumping through my veins. The steady beep-

beep-beep on the heart monitor picked up its pace. If I had been out of operation for *over a year*, that meant Number 1 and all the other alien outlaws roaming around Terra Firma had basically been enjoying a free ride, with no Alien Hunter to slow them down. I couldn't even imagine what kind of dirty deeds my nemeses had been up to in my absence, and as you know, I have a very vivid imagination.

I decided I didn't have a choice.

I needed to get out of this hospital as quickly as I could and resume my duties as the planet's protector.

So I did what had to be done.

I had to confess who I really was and what I could really do.

"Okay," I said, "this is going to sound extremely strange. You might even think I'm a little insane. But hear me out."

Every medical professional in the room was staring at me like I was nuts.

"I'm an alien."

Okay. Now they were staring at me like I was loonier than a tune.

"Excuse me?" said Dr. Oz.

"I came to Earth from Alpar Nok."

"And where, or what, is that?"

"It's a planet. In a galaxy far, far away."

"Like in *Star Wars*?"

"Exactly!" Good. They understood. "I came here to

protect your planet from other, evil aliens and—well, not to brag, I have incredible powers."

"Like Superman?" said Dr. Gupta. "I believe he came to Earth from a distant planet as well."

"True, but Superman's just a comic book, Doc. I can actually do things."

Dr. Gupta arched an eyebrow. "Really? And what exactly can you do, Daniel?"

"Lots of stuff. Okay, your stethoscope? I can turn it into anything you want."

"Really?"

"Yeah. I can rearrange matter at the atomic level."

"Well, Danny Boy, I'd like a diamond necklace," said Nurse O'Hara, tapping her stethoscope. Her smile had slipped into a sarcastic grin. "From Tiffany's."

"Fine."

Hey, if I had to perform a few quick parlor tricks to earn my ticket out of this place, I was game.

I concentrated on the shiny knob at the end of Nurse O'Hara's stethoscope. I figured I'd turn it into the Hope Diamond. That's a 45.52 carat deep-blue gemstone, housed in the Smithsonian, that some say is worth a quarter of a billion dollars. A little over the top? Sure. But I needed to prove my point, fast.

I focused hard. I even squinted.

But nothing happened.

Nurse O'Hara *tsked* her tongue.

Fine. If these people wouldn't let me out of the hospital,

I'd teleport myself out of the place. I'd zoom off to London, maybe Paris, or Tokyo.

Only that didn't work, either.

Dr. Oz took a step toward the bed. "Daniel..."

I shot up my hand and stretched out my fingers.

"Don't come any closer, sir. I've just put up a pulsating electromagnetic force field."

"Is that so?" He took another step. Nothing happened.

I was definitely starting to freak. Something was seriously wrong. Had all my powers seeped away while I was out for the coma count?

"Wait," I sputtered. "I've been lying in this bed too long. My powers have atrophied.... Weakened. But they'll come back. You'll see. Tomorrow. Maybe the next day. I'm not really sure because I've never experienced a *total* power drain before. Usually, there's a residual..."

Two burly orderlies the size of linebackers barged into the room.

Dr. Oz nodded toward my bed.

"Young Daniel here needs his rest."

Remember how the doctor had reached into his pocket? I'm guessing that's when he'd summoned the security goons.

"No, wait," I said to the two no-neck body builders. "I'm warning you...."

The big men lunged toward my bed.

I had no choice. I didn't want to hurt the muscle-bound bedpan boys, but when I'm attacked I instinctively fight back.

But I couldn't budge.
The two men pinned me down.
Dr. Oz jabbed a hypodermic into my thigh.
I yelled out once.
Then I swirled down a rabbit hole of darkness.

Chapter 3

SOMETIME LATER (I just hoped it wasn't another thir-teen months), I was able to open my eyes again.

It was my turn to smile.

Much to my relief, my home buds from the planet Alpar Nok—Willy, Joe, Dana, and Emma—were standing in my hospital room. They were my best friends since forever.

"You guys," I whispered. "This is awesome. Thanks for coming!"

Apparently, my subconscious had summoned my four friends during my deep, drug-induced sleep, because in my current predicament being *alone* wasn't the best move.

Oh, one thing you need to know: When I say I sum-moned my friends I don't mean like a rich guy summons his butler by ringing a dainty little dinner bell. I mean that I conjured them up. Joe, Willy, Dana, and Emma are now one-hundred-percent purely products of my imagination.

Hang on. That doesn't mean I spend my time talking to people who aren't there. When they're around, everybody can see them, hear them, and, in Joe's case, smell 'em. (What can I say? The guy loves chili dogs. With cheese and chopped onions.)

The real Joe, Willy, Emma, and Dana are all dead, which meant I would've been flying solo in your world if it wasn't for my incredible ability to manipulate atomic nothingness and turn it into the best friends a guy ever had.

Seeing the four of them huddled around my bed in that hospital room made me feel totally pumped. For one thing, I knew I'd have backup when I took on Number 1. For another, if my friends had materialized for me, that meant my creative juices were flowing again.

"You guys," I said. "You have no idea how good it is to see you!"

"Same here," said Joe. "Now that you're awake, maybe they'll bring you some real food instead of dripping beige gunk down your nose through a tube. I could really go for a gallon or two of chocolate milk. And how's the pizza in this place?"

I grinned. My friend Joe? His stomach is a bottomless pit.

"It's a hospital, Joe," said Dana, who—just to bring you up to speed—is my dream girl and soul mate. More about that later. Trust me, it gets complicated. "They only serve Jell-O and cottage cheese."

"Why?" said Joe. "Don't they want anybody to get better?"

"You guys?" I said. "Can we talk about food later? I've got work to do. You need to help find my laptop—The

List." I hadn't seen my backpack with the alien supercomputer since my accident. It had critical info on all the alien outlaws on Earth, including The Prayer. I couldn't hunt him without it.

"I know," said Emma, the gentle earth mother of my gang. "The school's been keeping a list for you, and it doesn't look pretty. A whole year's worth of homework." She shuddered in fear.

"And math?" said Willy, the group's natural-born leader. "It got ugly this year, Daniel. It turned into calculus!"

I was confused again.

"Willy, what are you talking about? I need to take care of Number 1."

"Okay, where's your bedpan?" asked Joe.

"Great, you guys," said Dana, rolling her eyes. "I *so* want to witness Daniel's bodily functions at work."

"Don't worry about the homework," said Emma. "You'll catch up, Daniel. You've always been the smartest kid in class."

"Except riding your motorcycle in the rain," said Joe. "I'm sorry, I don't mean to bust your chops, buddy, but that was just dumb."

I shook my head. Tried to clear out the cobwebs left over from whatever drug Dr. Oz had needled into me.

I noticed a bunch of GET WELL SOON! balloons tied with ribbons to the foot of my bed.

"All right, kids," said Nurse O'Hara as she marched into the room. "We don't want to wear Daniel out. He's had a rough night...."

"Aw," moaned Willy. "We just got here...."

"Yeah," said Emma. "And Daniel just woke up."

"Out, the lot of you," said Nurse O'Hara. I noticed she was smiling again. "Don't you kids have homework to do?"

"Yeah," groused Joe. "High school's a beast."

"High school?" I said. "Willy?" I motioned for him to move closer so Nurse O'Hara wouldn't hear what I said next. "I don't go to high school."

"Well, duh."

I breathed a sigh of relief. I wasn't going nuts.

"You've been in a coma," Willy went on. "But now that you're awake, your butt'll be back in homeroom before you know it."

Chapter 4

MY STRANGE DAY kept getting stranger.

My next little surprise? An unexpected visit from my family—my mom, my dad, and my little sister, Brenda.

Quick recap, just so we're all up to speed here: *I don't have a family anymore.* I am, basically, the galaxy's number one orphan. As you already know, The Prayer murdered my mother and father when I was just a kid. He also masterminded the near-genocide of my home planet, Alpar Nok.

Is it any wonder the repugnant insect freak is the top target on my List?

Anyway, in the past I've been able to summon my mother and father back into temporary, artificial existence, just like I do with my four friends. In fact, my mom and dad were even easier to conjure than Joe, Willy, Dana, and Emma. And sometimes, like whenever I needed them most, my mom and dad just appeared.

But during my battle with the demon Abbadon (Number

2 on The List), I cast the ashes of my father and mother's immortal souls to the four winds. They can't come back to help me anymore, no matter how much help I might need.

As for my little sister, Brenda?

She's definitely not real. How could she be? She was never even born.

When Number 1 killed my mom, she was pregnant with the baby that would have become my little sister. That's right—The Prayer snuffed out my mother's life as well as the little life growing inside her.

Brenda, aka Pork Chop, never actually existed except in my imagination.

"Oh, Daniel," said the woman who looked like my mother. She was tall, blond, and pretty. She was also weeping. "You came back to us! "

"We were so worried," said the man who looked remarkably like my father. "We thought we'd lost you. Our house hasn't been a home without you, son."

"Actually, I thought our home was pretty awesome while you were gone," said the girl who was supposedly my sister. "I had the upstairs bathroom all to myself."

"Pork Chop!" said my mother, raising her eyebrows disapprovingly.

"Sorry," said my annoying li'l sis. "I'm just joking, Daniel. I really, really missed you, too. *Not!*"

I couldn't take it anymore.

"Who are you guys?" I said.

My father grinned. "That's an odd question, Daniel. We're your family."

"Don't you recognize us?" My mother's voice was quavering.

"He's still a little groggy," explained Nurse O'Hara, who had come into the room to adjust my IV bags. "It's to be expected. He's been unconscious for over a year. Who knows what sort of wild dreams he might've had while he was under?" She tapped the side of her head.

Yeah, Nurse O'Hara thought I was nuts. I guess I should've felt insulted but I didn't.

Mostly because I was starting to think the same thing.

My father sighed. "We've spoken to your doctors, Daniel."

"Did you really tell them you were from another planet?" my little sister said with a laugh. "I guess that would explain why you dress like such a dork."

"Pork Chop!"

"Sorry, Dad."

"Okay," I said. "You guys tell me. Who am I?"

"You're our one and only son, Daniel," said my mother, taking my hand in hers. "You are Daniel Manashil. You go to high school. You have four amazing friends...."

"One of them's your girlfriend, *Dayyy-na!*" said Brenda in a singsong voice. "Well, she *was* your girlfriend before you were stupid enough to ride your motorcycle in the rain. Now I think Dana might be dating Willy."

"What?" I said.

"Well, you can't expect her to wait forever...."

"No. What are you people talking about? I don't *go* to high school...."

"Let's take it easy," said my father soothingly. "You just came out of a coma, after all. You had a terrible accident, son."

"Really?" I stammered, not knowing who or what to believe. "What happened?"

"You were riding your motorbike home from school. A rainstorm hit. The surface of the road became slippery. You lost control and spun out, Daniel. Your bike skidded across the highway and slammed into a tractor-trailer truck. You almost died!"

"Actually," said Nurse O'Hara, "he *did* die."

Chapter 5

NURSE O'HARA KEPT fiddling with the tubes and wires attached to the equipment beeping all around my bed.

"You flatlined, Daniel," she said, tapping the monitor tracking the peaks and valleys of my heartbeat. "You had no pulse for two or three minutes."

"That means you could have had *serious* brain damage!" blurted my baby sister. "So now you'll probably dress even worse!"

"Brenda!" said my mom. "Honestly."

"What? It explains why Daniel thinks he's some kind of superhero from outer space. There was no oxygen in his brain for…"

"All right, everybody," said Nurse O'Hara. "Visiting hours are over. Young Mr. Manashil needs his rest."

For a second or two, I wondered who she was talking about.

Then I remembered: Everybody in the room kept

insisting that I was Daniel Manashil, ordinary high school kid. If that was true, then Daniel X was the biggest figment of my imagination (or anyone else's) ever!

What about all the incredible stuff I've done during my time on Earth? All the aliens I've battled, the human lives I've saved? I could remember enough nonstop action to fill four, maybe five books. Was all of that just a complex dream created by my poor, oxygen-deprived brain in the two or three minutes I was dead?

My family, the Manashils, promised to come back tomorrow and left.

I sunk my head back into the foamy hospital pillow and closed my eyes.

I didn't know who I was any more.

Daniel X, the Alien Hunter? Or Daniel Manashil, the high school kid who dresses funny and stupidly drove his motorcycle on a rain-slick highway? Somehow, I drifted off to a fitful sleep. I think they were still pumping sedatives into my blood system.

"Daniel?"

I opened my eyes.

A bearded man in a tweed jacket was sitting in a chair he had pulled up beside my bed. His fingertips formed a tent underneath his nose.

"Hello, Daniel. I am Dr. Loesser. One of this hospital's many licensed psychiatrists."

I nodded. I felt like I was teetering on the brink of insanity. Maybe a shrink was what I needed.

The psychiatrist stroked his goatee. "You are, most

likely, feeling quite confused. You have experienced a terrible traumatic shock."

He was right. Waking up in this hospital bed had probably been the most traumatic experience of my life—almost worse than seeing my parents slain by a giant purple bug with dreadlocks.

If, you know, any of that ever really happened.

I swallowed hard. "Am I crazy, doc? Because I kind of feel like I'm going nuts here."

He grinned. "No. Of course not, Daniel. You have simply spent your comatose time constructing a complex coping mechanism to ease the emotional pain of your poor judgment."

I must've frowned or looked confused.

"Allow me to explain," said the psychiatrist. "Nurse O'Hara has told me about your outburst with the doctors who came to visit you several days ago."

That was several days ago?

"She also told me the details of the fantasies you have discussed with your friends and family."

"Fantasies?"

"These stories about being an alien; how you were sent to Earth to protect all mankind."

"I'm the Alien Hunter."

The psychiatrist's grin grew wider. "Yes. So I have heard. Imagination and hallucination can be wonderful survival tools when one is unconscious."

"So I made all this stuff up? Just to kill time while I was in a coma?"

"That is one way to put it, I suppose. But let us look at some of the specific details of your 'story' more closely. For instance, this business with the…" He looked at a clipboard in his lap. "Ah, yes. 'The six-and-a-half-foot-tall praying mantis with the dreadlocks.'"

"They call him The Prayer."

"They?"

"It's his alias. On The List of Alien Outlaws on Terra Firma."

The shrink nodded. "Again, Mr. Manashil, I applaud your imaginative mind on the intricate layers of detail you have constructed to support your grand delusion. You say this creature from another planet—The Prayer, as you call him—killed your parents at your farmhouse in, let me see, Kansas?"

"Right. Back when I was three years old."

"Ah, yes. You were a mere toddler. A weakling. There was absolutely nothing you could do to stop the hurt and pain inflicted upon your poor mother and father by this horrible 'monster.' Don't you see what this dream is really all about, Daniel?"

I shook my head.

"Your own compensatory feelings of guilt and remorse."

"Really? I don't get it. What do I feel so guilty about?"

"Disobeying your parents, of course. Riding your motorcycle in the rain after they had repeatedly warned you not to do so. Your accident and near death inflicted tremendous hurt and pain on them, Daniel. Therefore, in your fantasy, to absolve your own guilt you created this horrible, alien beast. *You* didn't hurt your parents. 'The Prayer' did."

I didn't know what to say.

"Daniel?"

"Yes?"

"Do you remember the helmet you were wearing when you had your motorcycle accident?"

"No, sir."

The psychiatrist glanced down at his notes. "According to the police report, it was a Nitro *Mantis* Touring Helmet."

I swallowed. "Is that where I got the idea to make my monster a Praying *Mantis*?"

"Perhaps. What do you think, Daniel?"

I didn't answer.

I was too devastated, too confused.

Was my life as I remembered it nothing more than a grand illusion I'd concocted because I felt bad about breaking my parents' bike-riding rules?

How could that be?

It had all seemed so real.

So unbelievably, painfully real.

Chapter 6

LATER THAT NIGHT as I lay in bed, staring up at the ceiling tiles, wondering what kind of toppings Daniel Manashil liked on his Papa John's pizza or Coldstone sundae, it dawned on me.

Something was seriously wrong.

And it had nothing to do with pizza or ice cream.

It was this place.

I kept replaying Dr. Loesser's psychobabble in my mind.

Back when I was Daniel X (instead of some ordinary high school schmo named Daniel Manashil) I had the equivalent of a four-channel, XLR-balanced, +48V phantom-power digital recorder scrolling in my head at all times. I could, as they say when you call a tech-serve line, monitor my memories for quality assurance purposes.

I couldn't do it when I first woke up, but now that ability had returned.

Because I was still Daniel X!

Hey, how else could I have a Dolby Digital memory track of every word ever spoken to me?

I quickly scrubbed backward and replayed a chunk of the shrink's opening remarks:

Nurse O'Hara has told me about your outburst with the doctors who came to visit you several days ago. She also told me the details of the fantasies you have discussed with your friends and family...this business with the...Ah, yes. 'The six-and-a-half-foot-tall praying mantis with the dreadlocks.'...You say this creature from another planet—The Prayer, as you call him—killed your parents at your farmhouse in, let me see, Kansas?

I stopped the playback.

I didn't need to hear any more.

"Busted, Dr. Loesser," I whispered to myself.

I definitely couldn't shout it out loud. My hospital room was, undoubtedly, bugged.

Because here's the deal: I never mentioned *anything* about my family massacre in Kansas to anybody in this so-called health care facility.

How can I be so sure?

Easy. I was so emotionally scarred on that horrible day I rarely (if ever) talk about it to anyone. I certainly don't give up juicy details like the thing's dreadlocks to total strangers wearing white lab coats.

Yeah, yeah. I know. I should probably open up more. Let it all out. If I keep my emotions bottled up inside too long, I'll eventually explode in some kind of socially unacceptable manner.

Fine. Point taken. But I could work on that little personality quirk with a *real* psychiatrist once I busted out of this prison.

Because that's what this phony hospital had to be: the Alien Outlaws' prisoner of war camp.

And I had a pretty good idea who my warden was: Number 1.

Chapter 7

I DECIDED IT was time to die again.

Or at least to make it look that way.

Encouraged by the return of my mental recording mechanism, I was pretty confident that more of my internal powers would eventually come back. I might be able to rearrange the matter inside my own body because it was in such close proximity to my brain.

I wouldn't have to strain myself too much. I just needed to do enough organ manipulation to pull off a quick (and convincing) heart rate reduction.

On planets across the cosmos, the bigger the creature, the slower its resting heart rate. Great whales, the largest animals on Earth, operate on about seven beats per minute. The average heart rate for a sixteen-year-old earthling boy? Between 143 and 173 beats per minute. This is probably why those guys can't sit still for very long.

Anyway, on Sreym, a planet I visited once, I met this HUGE under-ice dweller called a freejinn. It's the size of

Rhode Island and lives in the darkness six miles beneath the glaciers that coat Sreym's polar ice caps. Its heart rate? Two beats every hour, like clockwork.

And the freejinn taught me how to do it.

I took a deep breath and concentrated hard. In my mind, I became a freejinn at the bottom of the Sreym sea.

I could still see and hear everything in the room, including the long, piercing screech of the EKG machine as my pulse dropped off the charts.

"Code Blue!" I heard a robotic voice call out from a ceiling speaker. "Code Blue!"

The two burly orderlies bustled into the room. Nurse O'Hara stormed in right behind them.

"What's going on?" she demanded.

"He's flatlining!" grunted one of the orderlies. When he spoke, a long, rubbery lizard tongue spooled out of his mouth. As I suspected, my orderlies were actually undercover aliens in cheap human suits.

Nurse O'Hara grabbed my wrist as the EKG machine continued screaming its annoying *beeeeeeeeeeep*.

"No pulse," she reported.

Well, that wasn't entirely true. My heart had already done its freejinnian ba-boom-boom for the hour. It'd be back with another drum solo in about sixty minutes.

"The Prayer must have his prey! We must resuscitate the boy!"

Note to self: it's pretty impossible to say all the "s" sounds in the word "resuscitate" when you're wearing a rubbery mask to make you look like a sweet Irish nurse.

My alien caregivers were so busy—frantically hauling me out of the hospital bed, sliding me onto a gurney—that they didn't seem to notice that their lip, nose, and eyeholes were sliding around to reveal blotchy patches of their true snot-yellow and puke-green skin.

"The Alien Hunter must not die!" cried Nurse O'Hara as the orderlies rolled me up the hall.

"Yes, Mistress," grunted the two orderlies. Slobbery gobs of gelatinous fish-gut goop dribbled out of their nose holes.

"Take him to the resuscitation chamber."

"Yes, Mistress."

In my self-induced state of suspended animation, I could still see and hear everything as they rolled me out the door.

The hospital corridors looked like the backstage of a movie set. The walls of my room had been made out of painted canvas stretched across wooden frames.

Without moving my eyeballs (dead guys don't do eye rolls), I activated my zoom vision and peered over my toes.

To the double door we were about to bang through.

When the foot of my gurney hit the exit bar, I smelled something decidedly delicious: fresh air.

The resuscitation chamber must be in some other building.

For the next couple of minutes, I'd be *outside* the prison walls.

Chapter 8

FURTHER PROOF THAT your nurse is actually an alien in disguise?

She whips out a Fearflash Stun Thumper—a wireless electroshock projectile cannon which is standard riot gear on the planet Cohlanghoo.

This happened maybe ten seconds after I kick-started my heart back into the average teenage Alpar Nokian range, leaped off the rolling stretcher, and raced (with my hospital gown flapping open in the back) toward the nearest tree line.

Nurse O'Hara fired a stun blast that missed me by a mile. I figured the eyeholes on her human mask had slipped sideways and obstructed her view.

I dug down deep and jacked up my speed.

I was nowhere near my personal best, a sneaker-sizzling pace of 438 miles per hour, but even in my bare feet I was doing a one-minute mile. I raced for the dark edge of the forest ringing the extraterrestrial's makeshift POW camp.

"Stop him!" shouted the deep, rumbling voice of the creature that had been pretending to be my angel of mercy. "Incapacitate him immediately!"

An interesting choice of words, I thought. *Incapacitate: to deprive of ability, qualification, or strength; make incapable or unfit; disable.*

She (or it) wanted to disable me, not destroy me.

An army of guards swarmed out of the prison buildings. They were loaded down with jangling weapons, the kind you can't buy on Earth—even in Texas.

Lithium battery–powered electroshock charges were exploding in white-hot bursts all around me. A couple of Nurse O'Hara's hench-goons were firing old-fashioned Earth Tasers at me, too. I could hear their wire-tethered electrodes whizzing through the air and ripping through the foliage around me. Some of the barbed darts thunked into tree trunks. One needle-nosed projectile nicked the side of my knee, delivering a quick jolt of what the Taser folks call "neuromuscular incapacitation." The sharp shock of fifty thousand volts delivering maybe half an amp of raw, electrical power momentarily interrupted my brain's ability to control my muscles.

My knees buckled.

Momentarily. Because I've studied enough physics to know it was the amperes and not the megavolts I had to worry about. Amps are what can blow circuit breakers or short-circuit your brain.

My nervous system quickly rerouted the excess amperage, sending the electrical energy rippling through my body's circuitry to recharge what, for simplicity's sake, I'll call "my batteries." In other words, the Taser hit was helping me regain power the way jumper cables help a car battery bolt back to life, or the way Red Bull "gives you wings."

"Thanks for the boost, boys," I said over my shoulder as I ran even faster through the thick trees.

A Fearflash Stun charge detonated maybe ten feet to my left. I quickly juked right.

Where another stun blast flared.

I dodged back to the left.

That's when I realized: Nurse O'Hara and her riot-squad goons were trying to prod me toward wherever it was they wanted me to go.

They were herding me the way cowboys herd cattle.

"Do not kill the boy!" the nurse creature screamed again. "His death has already been claimed by our Lord and Master!"

More explosions rocked the woods. I instinctively reacted to each one, changing my course to avoid the blowback.

Which suddenly stopped.

There were no more electrical eruptions. No more flash-boom explosions. All I could hear was my own rapid breathing.

Was the cattle drive over? Was I cornered in some kind of invisible corral?

I soon had my answer.

"RELEASE THE HOUNDS!" screeched the all-too-familiar voice of my mortal enemy. "Let the hunt begin!"

The Prayer.

Number 1, Nurse O'Hara's so-called Lord and Master, had come to claim his kill.

Chapter 9

I STARTED RUNNING again.

Out of the woods.

Down an embankment.

To a deserted highway.

Sharp chunks of gravel and shards of broken glass bit into the soles of my bare feet.

But I kept running.

I had no idea where I was headed except away from IT. Away from Number 1—the monster that so desperately wanted to finish what he had started all those years ago back in Kansas. He had wanted to kill me when I was three. He clearly wanted to kill me now.

"LET THE HUNT BEGIN!"

His battle cry rang in my ears.

Fortunately, whatever drugs the quack doctors had pumped into my Alpar Nokian system were starting to wear off. I realized what the "hospital" actually was: not exactly a POW camp but a high-end hunting club for the most twisted extraterrestrial ever to set his crooked foot on planet Earth.

Some earthling hunt clubs like to fatten up pheasants, geese, and ducks and then release them into their private game preserves. Doing so guarantees their high-paying guests a quality kill, not to mention a delicious dinner.

Nurse O'Hara and her minions seemed to be in the same business.

Fattening me up for the kill and warping my mind so their Lord and Master would be guaranteed a quality—as in *easy*—kill.

Forget hunting *him*. *He* was coming after *me*.

I ran a little faster.

A reflective green road sign up ahead told me the empty highway was I-94 and "Bismarck" was sixty miles dead ahead.

I was in North Dakota.

How did that happen?

That last highway I was walking along, right before the Mack truck rumbled over me, was in *Kentucky*.

I ducked into a rest area. Made my way from the parking lot across a patch of weedy grass to a picnic area.

I stopped running. And listened.

For The Prayer.

I scurried under a picnic table to hide. The way I hid back in Kansas.

I had been in the basement playing with my toys when the beast burst into our home. I fell to the floor when I heard a string of deafening explosions. "We love you, Daniel," my father had called out. "Always!"

And then I heard nothing except the clanging echo of the shots that had just killed both my parents.

Terrified, I knew the beast would come down into the cellar to kill me next.

So I squeezed my tiny body behind an old water heater. I tried to hide. Then I tried not to breathe.

"I know you're down here, boy," the giant insect said as his muscular legs clomped down the wooden steps. I saw him make a slow, horrifying roll of his stalk-like neck. "If you make me play this silly game of hide and seek, you are going to learn the meaning of the word *punishment*!"

Now, cowering underneath this old picnic table, I pulled my knees to my chest.

Was this it? My last hiding place? My final redoubt? Was our "silly game" about to come to very bad end?

I waited. My whole body trembled with adrenaline-induced palsy. And fear.

It was Kansas all over again.

Chapter 10

THANK GOODNESS FOR open-back hospital gowns that leave your butt hanging out in the breeze.

A sudden gust of cold air spanked my rear end so hard it shook me out of the little pity party I'd been throwing myself underneath the picnic table.

Snap out of it, Daniel! I said to myself, because—hey, somebody sure needed to say it. *You are Daniel X. The Alien Hunter. You're not a three-year-old kid hiding from monsters in the cellar anymore.*

And even when I was three, I wasn't a total wimp. I remember tricking The Prayer out of his third victim that day by turning into a tiny tick.

The memory made me smile for the first time in what seemed like hours.

Hadn't I been planning to take the fight to Number 1? Maybe his desire to hunt me down would turn out to be a good thing. It would definitely save me all sorts of time doing recon and gathering intelligence. I wouldn't need to track down The Prayer because I already had the perfect bait to lure him into whatever trap I set: me!

I quickly tested my external transformative powers by whipping myself up a new set of clothes, including shoes and a proper pair of jeans.

The jeans weren't perfect, a little baggy in the seat and totally *not* this year's hot style, but it was a start. My powers weren't functioning at the peak of perfection, but they were definitely on the mend.

I might still be vulnerable, but I was no longer *completely* defenseless.

I flashed back to when I was dealing with Number 2, a demonic alien who turned out to be the same creature earthlings have called Satan or Beelzebub. I remember asking my dad, "If Number 2 is the devil, what's Number 1?"

His answer still gave me chills: "Something much worse. He is a deity, Daniel. *A god.*"

So, to summarize, I—Daniel X—was currently being hunted by some sort of giant, all-powerful, omnipotent, insect-like god. One that clearly wanted to use some of its omnipotence to slay me and then destroy the adopted planet that I loved.

I was going to need backup.

Serious backup.

It was time to summon the real (and by real I mean imaginary) Willy, Dana, Joe, and Emma.

I focused on their spiritual essences.

Nothing happened.

So I focused again.

Nothing. Nada. Zip. I was still completely alone.

But not for long.

A big truck came rumbling down the highway. Its twin headlights cut across the darkness as it swung off the road and onto the rest area exit ramp.

I zoomed in on its front grille. Caught the glint of a sharply angled bulldog hood ornament.

It was another Mack truck.

The kind that nearly killed me in Kentucky.

And it wasn't alone.

Chapter 11

A CONVOY OF two dozen tractor-trailer trucks came rumbling off the interstate.

Pumping their hissing air brakes, they pulled into the parking lot ringing the grassy patch, which was dotted with picnic tables.

All twenty-four were Macks. All twenty-four had the same shiny chrome hood ornament: the tough, muscular bulldog poised to pounce.

I backed up a foot or two. I needed time to assess my situation.

The idling trucks, lined up in parking slots, more or less formed a semicircle of hot, thrumming steel in front of me. Behind me, I could hear a small stream gurgling through a ravine. If I ran across the open field and into the woods (again), the enormous trucks wouldn't be able to chase after me. They weren't what you might call "off road vehicles." They couldn't roll over me and crush my bones like that Mack truck back in Kentucky had.

I was about to make a beeline for the tree line when I heard The Prayer's disembodied, high-pitched voice echoing through the night. The beast was roaring louder than the thundering din of twenty-four diesel-powered engines.

"RELEASE THE DOGS!"

I expected rear cargo doors to roll up so twenty-four packs of braying, barking bloodhounds could come storming out of the big rigs.

I wasn't expecting a total transformation.

Every single trailer jackknifed up on its front and rear axles and morphed into a giant, muscle-rippled metal bulldog. The twenty-four trucks were turning themselves into twenty-four ginormous hood ornaments. Each powerful chrome beast had to weigh forty tons. They were forty feet long, fifteen feet wide, maybe twenty feet tall. Thick folds of shiny skin drooping down around their snubbed muzzles made them look angry at the world—or maybe just at me.

And these giant bulldogs had teeth.

Pointy steel bulldog teeth.

"SIC HIM!" screeched Number 1.

The giant dogs sprang up from their haunches and charged after me, their jagged metal paws clawing huge divots into the asphalt and chewing up sod like the teeth on a backhoe bucket.

I raced for the ravine.

Little known fact: Bulldogs were first used in Jolly Olde England for a bloody sport called bull baiting. A bull would be staked in the center of a ring. Bulldogs would be sent in to seize the bull by the nose (a bull's most tender part) and not let go.

Guess I was supposed to play the part of the bull.

Four of the gargantuan dogs broke off from the pack and leaped across the ravine in one easy stride on my right. Another four did the same on my left.

The Earth quaked when they landed.

The other sixteen beasts were snarling behind me. Silvery drool slobbered out of their jowls like liquid mercury from a shattered thermometer. Their job, clearly, was to run me through the brambles and bushes, and send me skidding down a slippery slope to the bottom of the ravine.

I was being hunted. Driven to ground, as they say in the fox and hound set.

I splashed across the shallow, rock-strewn creek at the bottom of the gulley and scrambled up the far side.

When I reached the top, the eight wide-shouldered brutes that had broken off from the pack were waiting for me.

The sixteen behind me bellowed and howled.

"TAKE HIM DOWN!" screeched The Prayer.

Eager to please its master, the leader of the Mack pack snarled in reply and leaped right at me.

Chapter 12

THE DINOSAUR-SIZED BULLDOG locked its jaws of steel around my body like I was its favorite tug toy.

When I wiggled inside its box-shaped muzzle, trying to work my way free, the giant dog shook its huge head back and forth to stun me into submission.

It more or less worked. I quit squirming. Made my body go limp.

Fortunately, the metallic dog's droopy jowls had flapped inward to blanket its sharp teeth so I didn't end up ripped to shreds with my stuffing strewn all over the ground. But the pressure clamping down on my body was excruciating. I felt like I was being squeezed inside an oversized vise grip. I could barely breathe.

"Bring him to me!" I heard Number 1 cry, his voice muffled by the jiggly walls of the giant bulldog's flabby cheeks. "Bring me Danny Boy, the little Alien Hunter!"

We were on the move. I heard the bulldog sniggering and snortling through its smooshed-in snout. I could feel its stubby front legs pounding down the ravine slope, through the creek, up the other side. Every step the forty-ton beast took rattled my brain.

I wondered if this slobbering silver hood ornament was part golden retriever. The obedient brute was bringing me back basically unharmed to its master, so Number 1 could have all the pleasure of killing me himself.

I thought about kicking out a few of my canine captor's teeth. But I knew I wasn't strong enough to take on a riled-up dog the size of a tractor trailer. Not yet, anyway. Chances were, if I lashed out I'd end up as kibble and bits. Lots and lots of bits.

I decided to go with Plan B.

Teleporting.

If I totally concentrate on where I want to be, I can send my body to all sorts of places just by using my mind.

Usually.

I wasn't sure it would work, if I had the juice to pull it off. But I had to give it a shot. Otherwise, Number 1 would be giving *me* a shot, and most likely it would be a plasma blast from an Opus 24/24, an alien weapon so heinous and cruel it's been banned across most of the civilized universe. The thing has a built-in molecular resonator that causes its victims to expire from pure, unadulterated pain.

It more or less tortures you to death.

Number 1 had used an Opus 24/24 on my parents. I figured he'd probably use one on me, too. Watching me die in a prolonged spasm of absolute agony would definitely give him the quality kill he so desperately desired.

I had to escape Fido's grip. Fast!

So I imagined myself safe and sound on a white sandy beach. I blocked out the stringy dog saliva sloshing around my ears and concentrated on waves lapping up against a sunny shoreline. Instead of smelling rancid chunks of Pup-Peroni rotting between the dog's teeth, I imagined palm trees gently swaying in a fragrant tropical breeze. The coconuts...

"Drop him!" commanded The Prayer.

The mammoth bulldog opened its mouth.

I slid down its slimy tongue and over the ridge of its teeth.

Tumbling to the dirt, twenty feet below, I rolled over on my back, closed my eyes, and focused hard on that distant beach. I imagined I was lying on a blanket, soaking up the rays, smelling bougainvillea blossoms.

I had to get there fast. I had to be there, now!

Because when I opened my eyes, I saw a giant praying mantis with blood-red dreadlocks standing over me. His eyes were glowing with satisfaction as he aimed the saw-toothed muzzle of an Opus 24/24 straight at my gut.

A squealing whine told me the weapon was fully charged.

Chapter 13

SUDDENLY I WASN'T lying on a beach or on the ground beneath Number 1's spiky feet.

I was standing in the middle of Times Square in New York City. Taxicabs honked their horns. Double-decker tour buses swerved sideways so they wouldn't run over me.

Because I was standing *in the middle* of Times Square—right on the dotted line between traffic lanes at Seventh Avenue and Forty-Second Street.

This was no day at the beach.

It was a night in bedlam.

I was stranded in a river of rushing traffic at the bottom of a canyon of towering skyscrapers, their sides cloaked in giant TV screens and blazing displays of neon light.

Yeah—my teleportation powers were definitely rusty.

They didn't take me where I wanted to go, but at least they saved me from a sure death back in North Dakota. Plus, I love New York City. The energy. The excitement. The spectacular light show that blazes across the skyline every night. It may not be the center of the universe as many New Yorkers claim, but it comes pretty close.

Suddenly a Mack truck, its chrome hood ornament glistening beneath Times Square's glare, came barreling down the avenue at me. My eyes zoomed in on the blocky, square-chested bulldog.

Would Number 1 really turn loose another of his forty-ton gigantor hunting dogs in the middle of New York City?

I wasn't about to stick around to find out.

I dove to the side, and landed on a traffic island crowded with pedestrians.

"Hey, watch what you're doing, pal," snapped a New Yorker. "I'm standin' here."

As the Mack truck rattled down Seventh Avenue, the truck driver yanked on his air horn to give me a serious blast of big city 'tude.

"Get out of the road, nut job!" he shouted as he flipped me a New York City–style single-digit salute.

I smiled and waved back—relieved to discover that sometimes a Mack truck is just a Mack truck.

As I stood huddled with the mob of pedestrians crowded onto the traffic island—all of us antsy for the light to change so we could charge across Forty-Second Street—my cell phone began to vibrate. It also emitted a very odd, very peculiar ringtone.

A ringtone I had never downloaded or heard before.

Chapter 14

THE TRAFFIC STOPPED.

The pedestrians froze.

The WALK sign never lit up.

All the giant billboards surrounding Times Square quit flickering, some with bulbs stuck in midblink.

Number 1, the all-powerful alien, the one my father warned me was a "godlike" creature, had somehow made time stand still in Times Square so he could send me a text message.

I glanced down at the screen on my Extremely Smart Phone (Apple will probably sell something similar in the year 2525). A glowing green message was waiting for me.

As I went to open the text, I noticed my hand was bathed in an eerie green glow.

I looked up.

I wouldn't need my phone.

The Prayer's message was boldly scrolled in bright green script on every conceivable electronic receptor in

Times Square. The jumbo-screen TVs. The flashing billboards. The chaser lights zipping electronic headlines around massive buildings. Even the illuminated advertisements on top of the stalled taxicabs proclaimed Number 1's message to me:

CONGRATULATIONS, DANNY BOY!
YOU HAVE MOVED UP TO THE TOP OF MY LIST.
YOU ARE MY NEW NUMBER 1.

I spent a few time-suspended seconds soaking it in.

I guess turnabout is fair play, as they say.

I've had The Prayer at the top of my list my whole life. Now it was his turn to make me his number-one draft pick, the prime target of his anger and wrath.

For a moment, I wondered who used to be The Prayer's Number 1. Why hadn't he focused on me in the past? Had he counted on some of his outlaw cronies in the Top Ten to take me down?

If he had, it didn't work out so well. I'd already erased numbers 2 through 9 before any of them could erase me.

So now it was just us.

Two number ones. Two Alien Hunters locked in what would be, for one of us, our final battle.

I was in for the fight of my life and I knew it.

And if I had any doubts about The Prayer's powers, they quickly evaporated when a pair of white-hot lightning bolts slammed into Times Square, blasting new potholes into Seventh Avenue and jolting time back into play.

The cratered asphalt steamed and sizzled. Sparks crackled like fireworks and spewed out of every sign and TV screen hanging over the crossroads of the world.

But the seen-everything New Yorkers around me just shrugged as the shower of electrical embers rained down on their heads. Some popped open umbrellas. Most probably figured a fuse must've blown somewhere. They just kept going to wherever it was they needed to be.

I stared at the smoldering holes in the street and shook my head.

Lightning bolts.

Apparently The Prayer had a serious Zeus complex.

Chapter 15

ALL THE RESIDUAL static electricity zizzing through the New York night air after the lightning strike gave me another power surge.

I could feel my nerves tingling, my senses sharpening.

I hoped it was the final energy boost my body needed to make my transformation powers fully operational. Because I really needed to turn myself into something other than a human teenager.

I didn't want to be a sitting duck. If the gangly alien known as The Prayer wanted to hunt an Alien Hunter, fine. Bring it on. But he was going to have to do some serious predator work before he could stick my taxidermied head on the wall of his twisted trophy room.

As you might remember, the first time I escaped from Number 1 back in Kansas, I turned myself into a tick. This time, I decided to become a creature that could survive anything the overgrown grasshopper dished out, including lightning bolts or a nuclear blast. An insect that can survive three months without food, one month without water.

I was actually glad none of my friends or family were there to see me do what I was about to do. It would've been even more embarrassing. Because I was sinking to a new low. Literally.

That's right. To lose myself in this crowd, I turned myself into one of New York City's most populous creatures: a *Periplaneta americana*, better known as the American cockroach. At a length of one and a half inches, I was the largest of the roaches you'll find in the Big Apple. My crispy shell was reddish brown with a yellow figure eight birthmark up front. I had wings tucked over my tail and a serious hankering for cheese, glue, flakes of dried skin, rodent corpses, and starchy bookbindings. I was also seriously disgusting.

I quickly clamped all six of my spindly legs onto the pants cuff of a guy climbing aboard a crosstown bus. I let him carry me up the steps, but as soon as he sat down I hopped off his pants, scampered down his socks, and scooted off his shoe right before he shook out his leg, feeling a creepy crawler.

I scurried across the sticky bus floor and, fighting the cockroachian urge to lap up a gooey brown pool of coagulated Coca-Cola, scampered between two very sensible shoes. I hid in the dark shadows underneath a row of scooped-out plastic bus seats.

I was safe.

For the time being, anyway. It was hard, even for a

skilled predator like The Prayer, to hunt prey he couldn't see, smell, or pick up on radar.

I twitched my antennae out my compound eyes and zeroed in on an advertisement displayed above the windows on the far side of the bus.

It was a poster for Roach Motels, those insect traps that use bait to lure cockroaches into a sticky-floored cardboard box. They squirm, starve, and eventually (after a couple of months) die. Since New York City is a multicultural town, the slogan was written in Spanish: *"Las cucarachas entran...pero no salen."*

I didn't need to activate my universal translator to know what the ad said: "Roaches check in, but they don't check out."

I just prayed the same wouldn't be true for me.

Chapter 16

AS I WAS CHECKING out the Roach Motel poster, a lady sitting directly underneath it was checking out *me*. When she saw my twitching antennae, she gasped and put one hand to her chest like she was having a heart attack. Her other hand was pointing straight at me.

"Cockroach!" she screamed.

Actually, it was more like a shriek.

"COCKROACH!"

Squirming frantically (and totally freaking out), she grabbed hold of a pole and clambered up it so she could *stand* on her blue plastic seat. Apparently she didn't want her feet anywhere near the floor of the bus in case I crawled on her.

"COCKROACH!"

My eye contact with the uptight, shrieking lady was broken when a man's size thirteen shoe stomped down a few centimeters in front of my twitching bug face. The shock of the shoe quake sent my two cerci tingling. (Cerci are the little hairs sticking out of a cockroach's butt that act like a motion detector.)

"Did you get him?" screeched the hyperventilating woman.

"Yeah," said the macho-macho man attached to the wingtip shoe. "I think so."

"Thank you," gushed the woman. "Bless you."

"No problem," said the guy, sounding like he thought he was Sir Galahad rescuing a damsel in distress.

I didn't want to break up their little mass-transit moment, but I also didn't want to spend another second gagging on the cheesy fumes coming out of the guy's socks and shoes. Unfortunately, cockroaches smell with their antennae *and* their mouths. I was taking in a double dose of sweaty foot funk.

So I scampered across the dotted toe of his wing tip.

"Roach!"

"Eeeeeek!"

"Cucaracha!"

Now everybody on the bus was aware of my presence.

I scurried down the center aisle, dodging shoes, zig-zagging around guillotining briefcases, barreling under swinging shopping bags, avoiding pointy-tipped umbrellas. These panicked people were using every weapon in their workday arsenal on me.

I raced through the gauntlet and made it to the front of the bus.

"Get outta here! Scram!"

Now the bus driver was getting in on the act. He was

trying to stomp on me with *both* of his heavy black work boots. I juked and jived, scuttled and scooted. The driver kept coming at me with both his feet—feet that should have been busy on the gas and brake pedals.

I could feel the whole bus swerving as the driver concentrated on the floor instead of the road.

I had no choice.

I had to lose the disguise or the driver would stomp me to death two seconds before his bus drifted into a head-on collision and killed all the passengers.

So I quickly transformed back into a teenage boy.

The driver's eyes nearly popped out of his head.

"Watch it!" I hollered.

He gripped his steering wheel just in time, saw the other bus we were about to smack into, and slammed on the brakes.

"Open the door, please," I said as politely as I could. "This is my stop."

When I heard the whoosh-thunk of the door swinging open behind me, I looked at the terrified passengers who had just witnessed a filthy cockroach turning into a normal kid.

"You're all safe," I said as reassuringly as I could.

But I couldn't help shaking my head and adding, "Seriously, people. It was only a bug. Grow up."

Chapter 17

I STUMBLED OFF the bus, totally wiped.

The passengers still on board looked dazed and confused. Most of them were probably wondering why they couldn't remember what had happened during the last five minutes of their lives.

The answer was simple: I had used my remaining creative energy to scrub their short-term memories clean. They would have no recollection of seeing a scuzzy cockroach turning into a kid who they probably thought looked pretty scuzzy, too. Hey, I'd been kind of busy. Grooming and hair gel hadn't been high priorities.

Anyway, I was exhausted from the mental exertion of mopping all those memories clean. And I was starving.

My crosstown bus had only crawled one block west so I was standing at the corner of Forty-Second Street and Eighth Avenue, right across the street from the Port Authority Bus Terminal.

Hundreds—maybe thousands—of people were scurrying in and out of the building. Commuters eager to head home to New Jersey and upstate New York. Friends meeting friends who had just climbed off suburban buses for a big night in the city.

I realized that's what I needed.

Not a big night in New York City; I needed my friends. Hey, the number one Alien Outlaw in the galaxy had just declared me to be his number one target. "Alone" was the last thing I wanted to be.

So once again, I tried to conjure up my four friends. And I didn't want the imitation Joe, Willy, Dana, and Emma who had come to visit me in the Hunting Camp Hospital. I wanted the real deals, even if they were one-hundred-percent purely products of my imagination.

I stared at clusters of friends greeting each other with hugs or helping with suitcases across the street at the bus terminal. I remembered sharing simple moments like that with my friends. Lending a hand. Being happy to see each other. Sharing that special bond you only ever share with your best buds. I totally grokked that warm, overwhelming sensation. Let it wash over me, knowing that what some wise earthling said years ago was absolutely true: "Friends are the family we choose for ourselves."

And then I heard a voice behind me.

"So, Daniel, where the heck is the *original* Original Ray's Pizza?"

It was Joe.

"I mean there have to be five bazillion pizza parlors in

New York City, all of them called Original Ray's, or Original Famous Ray's, or Real Ray's."

"The real one was just called 'Ray's Pizza,'" said Emma. "It was down in Little Italy on Prince Street."

"*Was?*" said Dana. "As in 'it's not there anymore'?"

"Yeah. Unfortunately, they closed."

"Bummer," said Willy. "I could go for a slice of pepperoni."

"Pepperoni?" groaned Emma, our resident vegan. "Do you even know what they put in that stuff?"

"Sure," said Joe. "Peppers and chopped *oni's*."

Willy laughed. Emma sighed. Dana rolled her eyes.

Me? I just grinned.

My gang was back.

"Hey, you guys," I said, "let's do a picnic up in Central Park."

"Um, Daniel," said Dana, "in case you haven't noticed, it's late. Isn't Central Park dangerous after dark?"

"Not if you have your friends to cover your back."

And, fortunately, I did.

Chapter 18

CENTRAL PARK IS this huge man-made forest in the center of New York City's island of Manhattan.

Approximately thirty-five million visitors tromp though its 843 acres every year. Very few venture in after midnight.

So my friends and I had Umpire Rock—a massive, mica-flecked outcropping just south of the park's Heckscher Ballfields—all to ourselves.

"So where's the grub?" said Joe, whose stomach needed to be sufficiently stuffed with food before it would let Joe take in the spectacular view of the skyscrapers ringing the park.

Feeling rejuvenated just by having my friends around, I felt confident I could whip up a feast. Maybe the entire menu from the original Ray's Pizza—everything from garlic knots to spaghetti to pizza pies.

"One midnight snack comin' right up," I said and materialized a heaping pile of steaming food on a red-checkered tablecloth.

Well, that was what I had intended to do.

Instead, what my imagination cooked up was a steaming pile. As in a trash heap.

"Um, Daniel," said Dana, "none of this looks very appetizing."

She was right. Instead of a smorgasbord of fine Italian dining, I had inadvertently conjured up a mound of chunky pig slop giving off gas vapors. It looked like that soupy stuff you see in the big rubber barrel in the cafeteria where all the leftover food scraps are collected.

"I think I'm going to hurl," said Willy.

"Good," said Joe. "It'll probably smell better than this mess."

Obviously, my matter-manipulation powers were still a little sketchy. They hadn't fully recovered from my quick-change cockroach transformation. However, I was able to evaporate the muck mound before it dribbled any farther across Umpire Rock.

"Don't worry, you guys," said Emma. "I have a whole bunch of vegan no-bake peanut butter protein bars in my backpack."

"Oh, joy," said Joe.

But he was hungry enough to eat whatever Emma dished up. So was I. And we both considered ourselves lucky that she wasn't hitting us with one of her famous raw power bars.

After everybody wolfed down about three bars each, Dana and I ended up sitting together on a patch of grass filling one of the crevices on Umpire Rock. The rest of the gang ran down to the nearby playground to check out the swing sets.

Like I said earlier, Dana is my dream girl—she is literally the girl of my dreams. Her long blond hair and beautiful sky-blue eyes, her ability to make my heart skip a few beats, even her incredible scent—all of it comes straight out of my emotional memories of the real Dana, the girl I knew back on Alpar Nok.

Dana was the prettiest and most grounded person I had ever met.

Until I met Melody Judge, the daughter of an FBI agent. Her dad heads up a secret government task force that deals with extraterrestrial outlaws. Melody reminds me so much of Dana, right down to the pale scar on both their cheeks, that I truly believe my soul mate from the planet Alpar Nok somehow found me again here on Earth.

Or maybe I just made that last bit up because I don't want ever to have to choose between the two.

Yes, when it comes to girls, I'm just like most guys: totally confused.

"So how's Mel?" said Dana, as if she had just been reading my mind, which she probably could since she more or less came out of it.

"She's fine. Safe at home in Kentucky."

"Yeah. I know."

"You do? How?"

"The same way I know you and Mel split an order of KFC's honey-barbecue wings two minutes before you idiotically decided to go for a 'stroll under the stars.' Along a deserted highway, in the middle of the night. Hello? What were you thinking?"

"Hey, I asked you to come with me." I quickly realized what I had just said. "I mean, I asked *Mel* to come with me. But she was wiped out. We'd taken the horses out for a really long ride."

Dana grinned. "Yeah. All the way down to McGimsey's farm. "

Okay. That was a stunner. How could Dana know what Mel and I had done back in Kentucky? Unless, of course, my imaginary friends have total access to all my memory tapes while they're hanging out inside my mind, waiting for me to summon them into action.

"Daniel?" said Dana. "Do you remember how I died?"

I nodded. Man, I hated talking or even *thinking* about this. "Yeah."

"And do you remember when that was?"

"Sure. Like it was yesterday."

"So you remember the date?"

"Definitely." It's still marked with a black circle on my calendar.

"Good. Then do the math."

"Huh?"

"Take the date of my death and factor in the time differential between Earth and Alpar Nok. Time moves much more quickly down here than it did back home, because of the shorter length of the solar orbit here."

71

"Wait a second. What are you saying?"

Dana smiled warmly. "The day I died, my soul found its next home—an Earth child, just about to be born. One destined to ultimately reconnect with my soul mate."

"Melody is you?"

"No. I'm Melody. Hey, you didn't think I'd leave you out here all by yourself, did you? What kind of soul mate does something like that?"

Chapter 19

AT LEAST I had one thing to feel good about.

The whole Dana-Mel-me weirdness wasn't so weird anymore.

Too bad Dana couldn't help me figure out an equally easy exit from my other jam: taking down Number 1 before he took *me* down. Mentally, I was kicking myself for not being better prepared to fulfill my primary mission on Earth as The Alien Hunter: destroying Number 1 for what he did to my family. For what he did to Mel's mom.

That was something else Mel and I had in common: she also lost her mother to The Prayer when the gangly beast went on his rampage back in Kansas.

So I had to stop Number 1, no matter what seemingly invincible powers he possessed. I had to stop him before he wiped out every mother, father, and child on the planet—starting, of course, with me.

"You're at the top of his list?" said Willy as we made our way out of Central Park.

Joe had used the GPS unit in his high-tech wristwatch (trust me, it does a ton more than tell time) to track down a nearby branch of famous original Ray's Pizza on Columbus Avenue that was open till three AM. The vegan protein power bars had only kept his stomach happy for maybe fifteen minutes. He was starving again.

"Don't worry, Daniel," Willy, my wingman, continued. "At least we won't have to waste time tracking down Number 1. He'll come gunning for you."

"That's what I've been thinking," I said as we came out of the park near West Eighty-First Street. "But I need a plan for when he shows up. I also need my full powers. How can I go up against Number 1, who can manipulate the space-time continuum *and* chuck lightning bolts at me, if I can't even whip up a few simple pizzas?"

"Your powers always kick in when you need them most," said Willy. "It's like your raw emotions mixed with the free-flowing adrenaline of a crisis become the rocket fuel that turbocharges your creativity."

"Besides," said Emma, *"we're* still here."

"That's right," said Joe. "You didn't turn *us* into steaming piles of puke like you did with those pizzas."

"He didn't?" joked Dana, sniffing the air near Joe's neck. "Oh. Right. That's just your natural body odor."

I shook my head and smiled. My friends were fun to hang with. They were also right.

My full powers would come back to me. Soon.

At least I sure hoped they would.

"Maybe *we* should take the fight to Number 1," suggested Dana. (I figured I should call her 'Dana' when she was imaginary; 'Mel' when she was living, breathing, and horseback riding.)

"Or," said Joe, his genius for strategy and tactics kicking in, "we let him *think* he's bringing the fight to us when he's just being lured into a giant bug zapper with Daniel as bait. Hey, speaking of bait, do you guys remember that sushi we had back in Tokyo?"

"I thought you wanted pizza," said Dana.

"Sushi would be..."

Joe did not finish that sentence.

In fact, nobody said anything for about ten seconds. We all stood frozen on the sidewalk, gawking at a huge, glowing sphere suspended in midair and surrounded by eight orbiting planets. Earth's entire solar system was only one hundred feet away, captured inside a glass box seven stories tall!

Chapter 20

"WHAT *IS* THIS PLACE?" asked Willy.

Joe's talking smart-watch gave us the answer. "Welcome to the American Museum of Natural History's Rose Center for Earth and Space and the Hayden Planetarium."

"This is where New York City keeps its stars," I remarked.

"I thought that was Broadway," said Joe.

"Not those kinds of stars," I said with a laugh. "*Our* kind. Constellations. Galaxies. Spiral nebulas."

"Daniel's right," added Emma. "There's too much light pollution in this city from all the skyscrapers and cars and flashing signs for New Yorkers to see the real stars. The sky never gets dark enough. So they come here to see the heavens splashed across the curved ceiling of that giant sphere."

"The Hayden Planetarium is the most technologically advanced space theater in the world," added the smooth-talking Tour Guide App in Joe's wristPod. "It presents hyper-realistic views of the night sky, as seen from Earth, using the world's most advanced star projector: the Zeiss Mark IX, custom made for the museum."

"Um, Joe?" said Dana.

"Yeah?"

"Can you turn that thing off?"

"Why?"

"Because I have an idea that I don't want *it* to hear."

Joe tapped a switch on his wrist gizmo. "Good-bye, Joe," it said as it faded into sleep mode. "I hope you find your pizza."

"Don't worry," said Joe. "I'm a man on a mission."

"What's up, Dana?" asked Willy.

"This is where they filmed that movie—*Night at the Museum*."

"With the dinosaurs coming to life and junk?"

"Yep." Dana turned to me with a sly twinkle in her eye. "So, Daniel—what's one of the best ways to get your creative juices flowing? To make sure all your powers are fully restored?"

I shrugged. "I dunno. I guess I could take a nap."

"Or you could do something way better. You could go inside the museum and play with all the toys. The dinosaurs and woolly mammoths. The Easter Island head statues, the big blue whale..."

"Um," said Emma, "you want Daniel to, basically, goof off when he's just been promoted to Number 1's number one enemy?"

"Exactly. A little creative playtime may be exactly what

77

you need, Daniel. You're *too* tightly focused. You need to loosen up, kick back, and let your imagination run wild. Face it—you need to have a little fun."

I realized Dana was right.

Sometimes the best way to solve a problem is to walk away from it for a little while and throw yourself into some completely different creative endeavor.

Like having a blast inside the American Museum of Natural History when no one else is around, except a few security guards, who I could easily mind-bend into taking a quick catnap.

It was definitely time for another "night at the museum"—Daniel X style!

Chapter 21

"I THOUGHT WE came in here to have fun!" screamed Emma.

We were being chased around the Fossil Halls on the museum's fourth floor by the petrified skeleton of a one-hundred-and-forty-million-year-old stegosaurus. The dinosaur had a row of guitar-pick-shaped plates running down its spine and jumbo-sized spikes on the tip of its tail.

"This *is* fun!" I had to shout to be heard over the roar of the giant dinosaur and the squeal of the baby stegosaurus that I had also imagined back to life.

"Watch out!" called Willy. "Triceratops on your right!"

This sixty-five-million-year-old dinosaur had three horns sticking out of its skull shield. All three were aimed at us.

"Third floor!" shouted Dana.

"Let's take the elevator," added Emma.

We dashed down a wide corridor just as a half-dozen fur-wrapped Neanderthals came running up it, carrying

spears and crude stone tools. They were waxy refugees
from a prehistoric-man diorama. Grunting at us to get out
of their way, they went chasing after the dinosaurs that
were thrashing around in the Fossil Hall.

"Maybe they'll make brontosaurus burgers," quipped
Joe. "Like the Flintstones!"

We jumped into a waiting elevator and rode down to
the third floor, where a cluster of chattering chimps, growling gorillas, laughing hyenas, howling lions, screeching
hawks, and a big honking Gila monster greeted us the
instant the doors flew open. Moments ago, they'd all been
stuffed taxidermy specimens frozen inside their display
cases lining the Halls of Primates, African Mammals,
North American Birds, and Reptiles. Now it looked like
they were ready to have a wild time on the other side of the
glass. A couple of primates started tossing plastic bananas
and monkey poop at each other.

"Um, how about we try the second floor?" suggested
Emma.

I flicked my wrist and the elevator doors instantly closed.

"Anybody know what's down on two?" asked Willy as
the elevator descended.

"Our Alpar Nokian friends," I said, because my internal Wi-Fi system was once again up and running, and I
had been able to access the museum's website.

We actually heard our otherworldly friends before we
saw them.

A blare of elephant trumpets greeted us the moment
the elevator doors started to open.

And there they were, from the Hall of Asian Mammals *and* the Hall of African Mammals: two herds of large, double-tusked pachyderms Or, as we call them up on Alpar Nok, our gift to the people of Terra Firma. That's right. Elephants—Asian, African, even the extinct mastodons—are aliens. Our Alpar Nokian ancestors brought them to Earth just to wow you guys about three million years ago.

After spending some quality time with the herd and taking an elephant ride through the museum's sweltering-hot live butterfly exhibit, we headed into what felt like home: The Rose Center for Earth and Space.

Joe cut donuts with a moon buggy he raced around and around the seven thousand square feet of the Hall of the Universe, directly underneath the giant Space Theater. The rest of us played dodgeball with the Willamette Meteorite, because I was able to levitate the 15.5-ton chunk of metal that had crashed into Oregon a long, long time ago from a galaxy far away.

Dana was right: playing was good for me. I felt as if *all* my powers had been restored, my batteries fully charged.

"Thanks," I said when the two of us had a moment alone in front of a 3-D image of colliding galaxies.

"Hey, that's what soul mates are for. Come on. Let's head upstairs. I'm feeling homesick."

"Yeah," I said. "Me too."

We all hurried up into the Space Theater where I activated the Zeiss star projector and sent us on a scientifically accurate virtual journey out of the Milky Way, across a couple of distant galaxies—all the way to Alpar Nok.

"It's beautiful," sighed Emma as our home planet drifted into view on the ceiling, surrounded by its familiar sea of stars—the same constellations we used to see when we were kids staring up into the peaceful night sky.

"It's awesome," said Willy.

"Totally," said Dana.

"Actually," groused Joe, "it could be even more awesome."

"What? How?"

"Well, there could be pizza."

And so I whipped up a killer pizza-fest. Ten different kinds. Everything from pepperoni to Hawaiian to veggie to cheese slices topped with french fries. Every pie was perfect. Everybody got exactly what they wanted.

"Okay," said Joe. "Now the stars and all that junk are spectacular. Stellar, even!"

We all laughed.

When the pizza was finished and we were all just quietly stargazing, I thanked Dana again.

And then, exhausted from the most fun I'd had in an extremely long time, I drifted off to sleep the best way possible—tucked in underneath a blanket of stars.

Chapter 22

MY MOST PEACEFUL sleep since getting run over by a Mack truck ended abruptly with somebody yanking at my leg.

"Hey, kid. Wake up. What are you doing in here? The museum doesn't open for four hours."

It was a security guard. One of the guys I had put into snooze mode so my friends and I could enjoy our night in the museum without any adult supervision or interference. I looked around the planetarium. The seats were all empty. The gang was gone.

"What the heck do you think you're doing in here, anyway?" demanded the guard.

"Well, sir," I said very contritely, "I was with my school group and I guess I must've fallen asleep during the star show. I hope I didn't miss my bus."

"Your bus? It's six o'clock in the morning. There aren't any freaking school buses outside."

"Really? Gosh. How will I get back to school?"

"Wait a second. Are you trying to tell me that you've been asleep in here since yesterday afternoon? How come I didn't see you when I made my rounds last night?"

I could tell the guard wasn't buying my cover story. He was also getting his grump on, big time. Probably because he didn't sleep very well last night. I guess I should've made sure he was sitting in a chair or lying down in a comfy mummy's sarcophagus before I put him under. It's never very comfortable to sleep standing up. Unless, of course, you're a horse.

"There's something hinky going on here," said the grouchy security guard as he reached for the radio clipped to his belt. I figured he was about to summon backup or a truant officer or maybe even the NYPD.

So, powers feeling fully functional, I employed a little Alpar Nokian mind trick and altered the guard's mental perception of "what the heck" was going on. It's sort of an instant hypnosis type of thing I do. And, yes, it can be a blast at parties.

"Oh, I see," said the guard, clipping his walkie-talkie back to his belt. "You got separated from your school group. But now you're going to walk out of the museum and take the subway home. That sounds like a very good plan, young man."

"Thank you, sir. Have a nice day."

"You too," said the guard, a placid smile on his face.

Actually, I just hoped my day didn't include getting stabbed in the back by a lightning bolt.

I decided I'd better check in with Mel's father, FBI

Special Agent Martin Judge, down in Washington, D.C. I needed to fill him in on the new developments regarding Number 1, the leader of all the alien outlaws on Terra Firma. Special Agent Judge headed up the government's Interplanetary Outlaw Unit, or IOU, which even *he* considered a lame name but couldn't change it. "It's already etched in the glass on my office door," he'd told me.

Agent Judge had also been one of my father's few earthling friends. They'd worked together, years ago, hunting down the aliens infesting Earth. Judge had lost his wife, Mel's mom, to The Prayer. For me, that meant the man had definitely earned the right to be included in my final alien hunt.

When I exited the museum, I ducked into a nearby dog run. The place was empty and secluded behind a hedgerow. I figured it would be the best place for me to teleport down to D.C. without attracting too much unwanted attention.

Usually, when I teleport it's instantaneous. There's no woo-woo music like on *Star Trek*. No glittering ghost image of my body as I fade out of view. I just focus on where I want to be and—*BOOM!*—I'm there.

Only not today.

Apparently, not *all* my powers were up and running.

Either that, or the omnipotent Number 1 was overriding my mental circuitry, bending my mind as if it were a warm Twizzler—doing to me what I had done to the security guard.

Whatever the reason, I wasn't able to mentally project

myself down to the nation's capital. So, once again, I tapped into my internal Wi-Fi to explore alternate means of transportation.

Flying commercial was out. Airplanes have to travel through the sky where godlike aliens typically hang out. I'd be an easy target trapped inside a metal tube hurtling along at thirty thousand feet.

I'd have to take the train. Amtrak.

But first I'd take the subway from West Eighty-First Street down to New York's Penn Station.

Because the subway was underground where there'd be a much lower risk of lightning strikes.

Chapter 23

DISGUISED AS A nerdy-looking college student (all I needed was a pair of glasses, a ratty knit hat, and some ironic facial hair), I hopped aboard Amtrak's fastest train: the Acela Express from New York to Washington.

Just before the train was scheduled to depart, a very cute girl about my age (and also wearing glasses) worked her way up the aisle, which was crowded with passengers stowing luggage in the overhead racks. She had a small backpack slung over one shoulder and stopped when she reached my row.

"Excuse me," she said with the most *mellifluous* voice I have ever heard, "but is that window seat taken?"

I quickly glanced around the train car. There were still plenty of empty seats—including whole rows that were completely vacant.

"No," I said with a smile, moving in so she could take the aisle seat.

As she sat down, I realized there was something special about this girl. An aura. She seemed to glow with calm confidence.

"I hope you don't mind sitting with me," she said, smoothing out her skirt.

"Not at all."

"I just thought you'd be a much more interesting travel companion than all these..." She lowered her voice to make sure no one could hear what she said next. *"Business people."*

That made me laugh. "I hope so. I'm Daniel."

"Mikaela," she said, extending her hand for me to shake.

The instant I gripped it, I felt a warm tingle flowing through my body. It shot all the way down to my toes. Yeah. Mikaela was definitely something special.

"So, Daniel," Mikaela said with a knowing grin, "where are you traveling?"

"Union Station, D.C. How about you?"

"The same."

"Do you live there?"

"Not really." It was kind of an odd answer, but she quickly reached into her backpack and pulled out a tattered and stained paperback. "Hey, have you ever read this? I found it at a flea market last weekend. *Stranger in a Strange Land* by Robert A. Heinlein. It's from all the way back in 1961."

"And it's still one of my favorites," I said, because it

was. *Stranger in a Strange Land* tells the story of Valentine Smith, a human born on the planet Mars who comes to Earth after being raised by Martians. Smith has to figure out how to live with earthlings on what he considers a very odd planet; he is the stranger in a strange land. It's probably the most famous science fiction novel ever written. It's also, basically, my life story.

"I really love this word the author made up," said Mikaela. "'To grok.' Do you know what 'grok' means, Daniel?"

"Sure. 'To understand so thoroughly that the observer becomes a part of the observed,'" I said, quoting Heinlein's novel from memory. "'Grok' is a Martian word that can't really be fully translated into any language on Earth."

"That's right," said Mikaela. "The closest we can come is 'to drink in.' Or maybe 'merge' or 'blend.'"

The train pulled out of the station, but I barely noticed the passing scenery. I was too busy "drinking in" Mikaela.

Like I said, there was just something about her. An otherworldly tranquility.

She flipped through the musty pages of her paperback.

"On Mars," she said, "water is scarce. When Martians drink, their bodies merge with the water, combining to make a new reality greater than the sum of its parts."

"Right," I said. "The water becomes part of the drinker,

and the drinker part of the water. Both *grok* each other. There's a duality."

"Yes," said Mikaela. "Dualism is a fascinating concept. One that might be good for you to remember."

"What? What do you mean?"

"Dualism. A state in which something has two distinct parts that are often opposites. For instance, the battle between good and evil."

"Right. But, why did you say it might be good for me to remember?"

Mikaela smiled warmly. "Because it might be. Would you like a Sprite, Daniel?"

"Um, no."

"I would. Excuse me. I'm going to the café car." She stuffed her book back into her knapsack. "You're sure I can't get you anything?"

"Positive. Thanks."

And then she headed up the aisle toward the rear of the train.

Mikaela never came back.

I didn't see her again—not even when we arrived at Union Station and I scanned the crowd on the platform with my built-in face-recognition software.

Maybe she got off in Baltimore or Delaware.

Unfortunately, even though I had liked her instantly, I didn't have time to worry about Mikaela, my stranger on a strange train.

I had places to be. Things to do. An evil alien to eliminate.

I also had two other girls to think about: Mel and Dana, who, I had recently learned, were one and the same.

Maybe that's why Mikaela and her paperback had been sent into my life for fifteen minutes. To help me grok the "duality" of *that*.

Chapter 24

AFTER BEING CLEARED through security at the FBI's Hoover Building, I was escorted down to Agent Judge's extremely secret office by two of his men.

"Good to see you again, Daniel," said one, a former Navy SEAL who had been with me on my mission to deal with Abbadon, the demon who'd been Number 2 on the list of Alien Outlaws operating on Terra Firma until we scratched him off.

In fact, this particular Navy SEAL had marched with me to the gates of Hell. Literally.

"Heard you had a situation in Kentucky," he said.

I arched a quizzical eyebrow.

"From what I hear," the SEAL continued, "you ended up looking like I did that time we went one-on-one in the ring: like you'd just been run over by a truck."

That made me smile.

The SEAL led me through a labyrinth of winding corridors and sliding doors made out of bulletproof glass.

Special Agent Judge's highly classified ask-and-we'll-deny-its-existence Interplanetary Outlaw Unit had its base of operations in the bowels of the Hoover building: down in the basement's basement.

Needless to say, the views out Special Agent Judge's corner office windows were lousy, unless you enjoy looking at slabs of gray cement.

"Mel is safe," he assured me when we were alone. "She's at the horse farm with Xanthos and a heavily armed security detail."

Xanthos had been my father's spiritual advisor and had recently served me in that same capacity. Xanthos was a horse, the most magnificent white stallion I have ever seen. That is, he *looked* like a horse. He was actually a friendly alien creature with the extraordinary ability to communicate telepathically. He hailed from the planet Pfeerdia where all the superintelligent creatures look like what we call horses and sound like what we call reggae singers.

In a weird way, Xanthos reminded me of Mikaela. He had the same sort of centered calm that I had picked up during our brief train ride together. Maybe they took yoga classes together.

"Daniel?" said Agent Judge. "Are you okay?"

"Sorry, sir. Guess I zoned out a little. I was just thinking. About stuff."

"Well, son, you have a lot of 'stuff' to think about, that's for sure. It's not every day that someone becomes the number one target on the number one alien outlaw's hit list."

"I can deal with it. In fact, having The Prayer hunting *me* might work out to our advantage."

Agent Judge nodded. "A lot less legwork on your part. You won't have to track him down if he comes looking for you."

"Exactly. I just want to make one hundred percent certain that nobody else gets caught in the crossfire."

"Maybe you should head back to the farm, Daniel. Check out the security precautions we put in place. Look for any weaknesses. I'm sure you'll see something we missed."

"Thank you, sir. I think I'll do that."

"Good." He clacked a few keys on his keyboard. "And while you're traveling to Kentucky, here's something else for you to kick around in that big alien brain of yours."

His computer screen filled with a Hubble Space Telescope image of a sea of stars, their flickering light distorted into double arcs swirling above and below a large magnetic cloud. At the center of the circular cloud—which had a faint, violet tinge to it—was a gaping black hole.

"Where was that image recorded?" I asked.

"Pretty close to home, as things go in this galaxy. It's only a couple of thousand lights years away."

"Could this anomaly affect Earth?"

"Definitely. Especially if it keeps growing at the pace it has been. It could destroy our entire solar system, not to mention a few billion other stars and planets clustered in the Milky Way. The guys at NASA tell us it's something they've never seen before. A new kind of massive, fast-growing, and highly dangerous black hole."

A black hole, of course, is a region of space-time with such intense gravitational pull that nothing, not even light, can escape. Black holes form when massive stars collapse at the end of their life cycles and grow by absorbing mass from their surroundings. By sucking in other stars and gobbling down planets.

"Earth could hit this black hole's event horizon in a matter of months. If it keeps expanding unchecked," said Agent Judge, "maybe weeks."

"Event horizon" meant the point of no return. The line where the gravitational pull from the core of the black hole would become so great that Earth couldn't possibly escape. The entire planet would be pulled into oblivion. Earth would be like a grape swirling down a drain into a gurgling garbage disposal.

"When did your scientists first observe this phenomenon?"

"It popped up about a month ago. On the same day you took down Number 2."

One thing you learn pretty quickly when dealing with the most deadly and dangerous outlaws in the universe: there are no coincidences.

The superbad black hole the NASA scientists recently discovered had to be connected to Number 1. Don't forget, the giant bug-faced goon has, according to my dad, "godlike" powers. That means he can mess around with the space-time continuum *and* the vast cosmos of space itself.

I needed something I still didn't have in order to go up against an omnipotent enemy like that: a solid plan of attack. All I had was my anger and rage. That's never enough, especially if your opponent can punch black holes through the fabric of the universe.

Fortunately, when I tried (once again) to teleport, I actually pulled it off. I zipped instantaneously from Agent Judge's underground bunker office to his horse farm outside Louisville, Kentucky. One second, I was envisioning the lush green Kentucky bluegrass, the white corral fences; the next instant I was there.

Only, the grass wasn't green. And the corral fences weren't white.

Both were charred black and smoldering.

Firebombs with searing blue cores were exploding all around me, spraying up clouds of dirt and debris.

The Prayer was still one giant mantis step ahead of me. He'd arrived in Kentucky first.

Chapter 25

I SAW ONE of Agent Judge's FBI security detail troops leaning up against a burned fence post. All the IOU guys on Judge's team carried alien weapons that their unit had confiscated in previous firefights with outlaw offlanders. This agent had an RJ-57 tritium-charged bazooka slung over the bloody nub of what used to be his shoulder.

I dashed over to administer first aid.

"Don't worry about me." He grit his teeth against the staggering pain. "Agent Judge's daughter—Mel—she's in the house. Go."

In a blinding flash, I used my matter manipulation skills to cauterize the agent's wounds and build him a new, stronger arm. Willy had been right. In the thick of battle, pumped up by adrenaline, my powers seldom let me down.

Fire kept raining down from the sky, as if someone was laying siege to the Judge's horse ranch by launching catapults loaded with barrels of flaming oil.

I didn't care. I was stoked and primed for action.

I grabbed the wounded man's RJ-57 and raced through chokingly thick clouds of smoke toward the farmhouse, topping my personal best running speed of 438 mph. The rubber soles of my sneakers smelled like tire-burning day at the town dump. Too bad. I could materialize myself a new pair—*after* I saved Mel!

While running at hypersonic speed, I fought against inertia to raise the RJ-57 to my shoulder. The bazooka was powerful enough to punch a peephole through the Hoover Dam. It might be strong enough to knock Number 1 out of Kentucky and up into Indiana.

Because I saw the long, grossly bloated body of the most dangerous alien outlaw on the front porch of the Judges' farmhouse.

He'd come crashing out of the door, his head swiveling from side to side, his liquid-black eyes bulging out of his small, almost shrunken head.

The freakazoid had Mel trapped between his spiked, raptor forelegs, holding her kicking feet up off the ground. He fanned out his wings and sent his tangle of slimy red dreadlocks whipping around.

"Let go of me, you overgrown insect!" shouted Mel, squirming in the horrid creature's grip.

"SILENCE!" screeched The Prayer. "You are *MINE!*"

From my vantage point behind some trees, I lowered my weapon. I couldn't take the shot. Not without blasting Mel into oblivion, too.

Just then, a white horse came galloping across the pasture, his snowy mane and flanks shimmering in a shaft of warm golden light that seemed to follow him across the open field. It was Xanthos! Racing toward the porch, he let loose a powerful snort, pushing himself to his limits.

"NO!" shrieked The Prayer. "Keep away! I have claimed this one for the darkness!"

Number 1 spewed a jet of gelatinous blue flame out of his mouth. It erupted in a fireball inches in front of Xanthos's thundering hooves.

Still, Xanthos didn't stop. He leaped over the flames and galloped straight for The Prayer.

But half a second before impact, Mel and the spindly predator disappeared.

Xanthos reared up on his hind legs and pawed his hooves at the empty air where they'd just been standing.

Mel was gone. Number 1 had taken her.

Apparently, *his* powers of teleportation were fully functional, too.

Chapter 26

DO NOT DESPAIR, *Daniel,* Xanthos said in my mind. *The beast will not harm Melody Judge. He will use her as bait. It is you he truly desires.*

I know, I thought back. *The Prayer recently proclaimed that I was his number one target.*

The horse rumbled up a laugh. *"Ah, ha-ha-ha. Perhaps I should be congratulating you, yah mon? You have become Number 1's number one. Ah, ha-ha-ha."*

Quick sidebar: if you ever hear a horse start talking to you with a reggae accent inside your head, please—as they say in TV commercials about prescription drugs with side effects that might include nausea, dry mouth, or sudden death—consult your doctor. I, on the other hand, have telepathic conversations with other life forms all the time. Elephants. Whales. Baby seals.

And like I said earlier, Xanthos is actually an alien, not an Arabian stallion. He came to Earth from the far reaches of what astronomers call The Dark Horse Nebula.

Boy, did those guys get it wrong.

Xanthos was white on white on white. Sort of like a rice sandwich on Wonder Bread with extra mayo and the crusts cut off.

Tell me something, I thought to Xanthos.

Certainly, little brudda. I will tell you anything... if it is permitted.

Number 1, The Prayer—he seemed to be afraid of you.

Perhaps he fears I would squish him under my hooves. Ah, ha-ha-ha.

Come on. I'm being serious. Why would an omnipotent creature like Number 1 run away when you came charging at him?

Who says he is all-powerful?

My dad. He told me that The Prayer was worse than the devil himself. He told me that the Prayer was a god.

Xanthos shook his head. *Ah, that Graff,* he thought. *Your poppa was never my best pupil, mon. I told Graff that The Prayer was a highly refined manifestation of eternal, omnipresent, and omnipotent evil. But there is good in this world, too, little brudda. Good equally as strong.*

Well, whatever he is, he's certainly more powerful than me. Or at least, he has been up to now. He seems to know what I'm thinking before I've even thought it; where I'm going before I've even decided to go there.

As if to prove my point, my cell phone started shrieking that eardrum-piercing ringtone I had first heard in Times Square.

There was no need to check the caller ID. I knew it was The Prayer.

I punched the speakerphone button so Xanthos could hear what the overgrown vermin had to say.

"Where's Mel?" I demanded before the creep could screech out a single syllable.

"With me," he bellowed. *"WITH ME!"*

Now I heard the slobbery slither of a long, wet tongue.

"If you hurt her, I'll..."

"SILENCE! I grow weary of this world. I grow weary of this game. You no longer amuse me, Danny Boy. I will make a trade. We will end this once and for all."

What is it you would propose, evil one? thought Xanthos.

"YOU AGAIN!" squealed The Prayer like a lobster someone just plopped in a pot of boiling water.

Apparently, Number 1 could hear Xanthos's thoughts, just like I could.

Of course he could. He had every one of my other powers, so why not interspecies telepathy, too?

"LEAVE US. This is not your affair!"

Xanthos didn't back down. *What is it you would propose?*

"That we END this. *NOW!"*

"How?" I shot back at the phone. I was gripping the thing so tightly my knuckles had gone white.

"We trade your EXCRUCIATINGLY PAINFUL death for this worthless little girl's life. It is up to you, DANNY BOY. Follow your conscience. I would—if I had one."

Chapter 27

DO NOT FALL for this, Daniel.

My spiritual advisor's thoughts on the matter were crystal clear.

I had just terminated the call with The Prayer. Told him I'd consider his offer; that he'd have his answer soon.

"Do NOT make me wait!" he had shrieked in reply. "I HATE waiting! I want what I want, when I want it."

"Just give me a little time," I said, making it sound more like a command than a request. "Hey, if it makes you feel better, freeze time where you are. Pull out that tired old time-stopping trick you used back in Times Square."

"*YOU HAVE UNTIL NIGHTFALL!*" he bellowed.

That's when I hit the END button and cut off the call.

I warn you, Daniel, thought Xanthos. *It is a trick. Your death for her life? Hah! Once you are dead and gone, what is to stop him from killing all the humans, as well as your soul mate, eh? And, he* will *crush her soul, Daniel. This I know.*

The thing you call Number 1 can make certain the soul you knew on Alpar Nok as Dana is lost forever, never to return.

You knew Mel was—is—my childhood friend, Dana?

The noble creature sighed. *There are many things we know which we cannot tell, my brudda. We are advisors, not spies.*

Well, what if I tell Number 1 that I'll make the exchange. Then, when I get to whatever location he selects for my execution, I turn the tables. I summon up my four friends and we lay down the hurt on him. We squash him like a bug on a windshield.

And this is your plan?

Do you have a better one?

Yes. Take care, my yute. Beware of darkness. For in the darkness, it is sometimes difficult to see where the good ends and the evil begins. Do not give sway to the negative way.

It was my turn to sigh. *You always say that!*

Because it is always true, my friend. You cannot fight hate with hate, or darkness with something darker still.

Please. Now I was practically begging. *Tell me something I can use.*

Fine. I will tell you who used to be The Prayer's primary target. Who has been number one on its list since that list was first created.

Who?

The earth and all its inhabitants. You, my brave little brudda, were but an irritant to it. A trifle for it to sport with. But when you would not 'behave' in its hospital...

You know about that?

Yah, mon. Much has been revealed to me. When you would not behave, you became its primary target. It knows it must eliminate you before it can destroy Earth. If it does not, you will undoubtedly use your incredibly creative mind to come up with a way to save this planet from certain annihilation in the looming black hole of its creation. Oh, yes. I know of this, too. How IT created the swirling vortex when you ended its amusement by eliminating Abbadon, the beast you called Number 2. So, Daniel, if you die, Mel and Dana and every other creature living on this planet will die soon after you. It will happen the instant this entire solar system is sucked off into the oblivion of its black hole.

It, I thought back. *You keep calling Number 1 an "IT."*

Because that is the thing's nature. It has no concept of right or wrong. No gender, no conscience, no soul. IT is nothing but pure negative energy and appetite. A predatory beast with a single-minded purpose: To hunt. To kill. To hunt and kill again.

So how do I defeat an IT?

By being true to who you are, Daniel X. By not becoming an IT, yourself. Remember, little brudda, you are much, much more than an alien hunter. You, my young friend, are now the earth's final protector!

Chapter 28

I QUICKLY MADE a command decision.

Without the aid of The List, I needed a new source for in-depth intelligence on my final foe. The List is the portable supercomputer that used to be my primary tool for up-to-the-minute information on extraterrestrial evildoers.

Why couldn't I just boot up The List again, do a few finger swipes, and check out Number 1?

Funny story.

My dad passed The List on to me after his death, but he didn't know that the miracle microprocessor was given to Earth's Alpar Nokian protectors by Number 1.

That's right. The guy at the top of the list was in charge of the list.

When my father passed over to the other side, he learned the truth. Then, in one of our "imaginary" visits, he shared it with me:

"For eons," he said, "this twisted creature we call Number 1 has been amused by the eternal struggle between good and evil; the never-ending battle of demons and angels, darkness and light."

"Destroyers versus creators," I added.

"Exactly. Number 1 has always favored the dark side, but more than anything, he enjoys watching a good fight between equally matched opponents. So, to keep things interesting, he pits the universe's finest creators against its deadliest destroyers."

So up to this point, all my adventures—and those of my father and mother who had started serving in the Alpar Nokian Protectorship long before I was born—had been extremely amusing to the giant freak we all called The Prayer.

Now, IT had grown tired of the game.

IT wanted our seemingly endless death match to come to an end.

Well, the feeling was mutual.

But first, I had to go back to the location of my first contact with the monstrous IT.

I needed to return to the scene of the crime. The setting that provided the fodder for my most hideous nightmares. The one place in the world I never wanted to visit again.

My childhood home in Kansas.

I needed to go there and find a clue, a hint, an answer— something (okay, *anything*) that could help me defeat Number 1.

Or at least survive.

PART TWO
HEADING HOME

Chapter 29

I REMEMBERED THE house being so much bigger.

Or maybe I had just been a whole lot smaller.

I had teleported without incident from Kentucky to what Number 1 once called my "pathetic little hovel in Kansas." My first home on Earth. That is, before it was burned to ground by a murderous lunatic. The empty lot was too depressing to look at, so I recreated the place as I remembered it.

It was a simple two-story white clapboard farmhouse, where I had lived with my mom and dad more than a dozen years ago. It was no McMansion, that's for sure. It had three bedrooms, upstairs and downstairs bathrooms, a wraparound porch, a detached garage, and a big basement. It was located in the middle of nowhere because "nowhere" is where Alien Hunters always need to live.

I walked around to the side of the house and studied the sheet of plywood nailed over what I remembered as the kitchen window. If you looked closely, you could see the scorch marks lining the perimeter of the plywood. This was where Number 1 had first exploded into my life with a wall-shaking detonation, taking my mother by surprise.

As I stood there, I heard her screams and sobs once again in my head.

And then my father's voice. *Wait, wait. Hold on. Lower the gun, my friend.*

But The Prayer hadn't lowered his weapon. Deafening, concussive blasts drowned out my father's voice. Agonizing blasts from an Opus 24/24. When the shooting stopped, my father called out the last words he ever spoke to me in the real world: *We love you, Daniel. Always.*

And then nothing. Just the clanging echo of the Opus 24/24 hanging in the silence.

I moved around to the rear of the house. My backyard. The place where I built my first model of Khufu's Great Pyramid out of sugar cubes instead of limestone blocks. I built it in HO scale (where 3.5 millimeters equals one real foot). I was only two-and-a-half years old at the time, but the pyramid was enormous and spectacular.

At least until it rained.

Now I saw the sloped cellar doors sitting like an aluminum wedge of cheese up against the house's mildew-stained foundation. I knew I could pull up on the handles, squeak open the double doors, and descend a set of rickety wooden steps into the basement, the place where I first encountered The Prayer.

I remember I was trembling and pressing my small,

vulnerable body up against an old water heater, petrified about what had just happened to my mom and dad, when a beam of violet-tinged light shone down the stairs into the basement. And then I saw it—a six-and-a-half-foot-tall praying mantis.

I sensed Number 1 was a shape-shifter, able to assume any guise he chose. I could do the same, although I wasn't great at it just yet, being so young.

As I reminisced, there was something about that awful night that seemed more vivid, more enhanced than I had ever remembered it before. I couldn't quite put my finger on what it was.

But it was something seemingly insignificant that I had seen in the basement as I hid behind that old water heater. It was some small detail that could be hugely important now.

Relax your mind, Daniel, Xanthos's thoughts reached out to me across the miles. *You can see more clearly when you let the visions come to you.*

There's something here, I thought back. *Something that will help me take down Number 1. I can sense it.*

It will come to you if you let it. Just as a revelation suddenly came to me.

What?

After you left, I drifted off into a very deep, very meditative trance, mon.

And?

I remembered something from the time long ago: I was not

your father's only spiritual advisor, Daniel. The man, he loved to have a backup for everything he did; a Plan B to go with his Plan A.

Okay. So who was this "backup" spiritual advisor?

This he never did tell me. But, I remember, he called her "his angel." She was your father's backup for me!

Chapter 30

XANTHOS GOT ME thinking: If my father had a backup spiritual advisor, what else might he have had a backup for?

How about the most important tool in his possession: The List? The computer that acted like an ultrasecret wiki about the superpowered psychopathic aliens that were plaguing Terra Firma. I'd lost it when I ended up in Number 1's hospital of horrors, and my chances of finding it now were less than zero. But if there was any way of learning Numero Uno's weakness—if he had one—it would be in The List.

Maybe some part of my father's extremely sharp mind realized that there was a remote possibility that the information he gleaned from the high tech computer might be compromised. That there could be a mole or a double agent working inside the highest levels of the Alpar Nokian Protectorship, feeding The List information for his (or its) own purposes.

No matter how far-fetched such a conspiracy, it would

still be—for my father anyway—what he called "a potential possibility."

And, therefore, he would have a backup. A computer he knew he could trust.

I walked across the yard and sat down in my old tire swing to think.

Focus, Daniel, I heard my spiritual advisor say. *Clear your mind. Concentrate only on what is important.*

I did as Xanthos advised. I blocked out everything except my internal search engine. It's like my own personal Google and it can find anything, no matter how obscure, that has made even the faintest impression on my long- or short-term memories.

"Search for computers," I said. "Alpar Nokian models and makes."

Knowing my dad, I figured he would have brought along his own personal computer when he went on the mission to Terra Firma. Maybe the trusty laptop he had used when he was studying at the Academy.

I added more layers of filtering for the search. "Portable. Extremely reliable. Made at least fifteen years ago. Able to communicate seamlessly across planetary broadband platforms."

And then I remembered my dad's favorite color.

"Orange."

In my mind's eye, I immediately saw a rotating image of a small prism tinted orange. It was made up of twelve five-sided glass panes. One pentagon served as the top, another as the bottom. There were two rows of five similar pentagon panels making up the sides of what looked like a miniature version of a Death Star.

It was the Tusk 5-12, a clever Alpar Nokian computer that linked communications, computation, and home entertainment into a single device the size of a paperweight.

According to my internal database, its primary component was a mineral called flervoniumide, which can only be found in the deep pit mines of Alpar Nok.

I extended my right arm straight out in front of me. I flipped up my hand and flexed open my fingers. I was transforming my palm into the high-precision search coil of a VLF metal detector. The kind of minesweeper you see being used by those dorks on the beach, searching for buried treasure.

Hand open and arm fully extended, I marched across the hardscrabble remnants of our backyard and into the woods behind our farmhouse.

The pings in my ears grew louder and closer together.

Soon I was hiking through the lush green grass at the edge of the salt marsh.

The pings became a steady beep.

I knelt down.

Pulled out a rooty plant. Scraped away six inches of muck.

And there it was. My father's emergency backup computer. Made of noncorrosive flervoniumide, with a battery that constantly recharged itself whenever it was within three feet of salty water. The Alpar Nokian Tusk 5-12.

I picked up the Tusk and studied the twelve animated screens.

One gave me the current weather conditions for Earth and several other planets. Another was running an old Charlie Chaplin movie. In a third, a text message scrolled across the screen. It was from my father:

"Hello, Daniel. I hope you are well. Remember, son, you must always have a backup. It isn't a weakness. It is a strength."

Chapter 31

HUNGRY FROM ALL my teleporting and tromping around in the woods, I returned with the Tusk computer to the backyard of my old home and quickly materialized a picnic blanket and a basket filled with food.

Nothing too fancy. Just all the foods I used to love to eat when we lived in Kansas: panfried chicken, Czech sausage, candied sweet potatoes, squash cobbler, German baked beans, Sunflower State wheat bread, and black walnut pie.

If there were any leftovers I'd save them for Joe.

When my stomach finally stopped growling after my second drumstick, I held the Tusk 5-12 in my hand as if it were a Magic 8 Ball and said, "What can you tell me about The Prayer?"

Every screen on the Tusk flashed to life with images and background information. I saw movies, heard audio clips, read classified documents, and then received what the computer called its "executive summary":

"The creature known as The Prayer, currently operating on Terra Firma in the guise of an oversized praying mantis, is the most evil alien outlaw of the current millennium. It has been responsible for countless deaths and untold destruction. Its planet of origin is unknown. Its powers have been recorded as 'unlimited.' It has no conscience, no emotions. It is pure evil incarnate. As such, it acts like a magnet, attracting lesser evil beings into its orbit of influence."

That's why The Prayer was at the top of The List. He was the godfather of the mutant mafia. The thing was bad to the bone, worse than all the other alien outlaws drawn to serve its overwhelming negative energy.

The Tusk computer kept downloading its executive summary. Things didn't get much better.

"Its area of infestation includes much of the galaxy known by earthlings as the Milky Way. It has also, in the past, orchestrated assaults on your home planet, Alpar Nok. Number 1's current danger rating is at the highest level. In numeric terms, it is listed as 99.99999. The creature intends to eradicate a large section of the known universe. Special abilities include telepathy, time-warping, Level 9 speed, Level 11 strength..."

Level 11? I thought. *There* is *no 11.*

"...shape-shifting, severe pain infliction, extreme cunning, overwhelming maliciousness, depraved indifference to life..."

I'd heard enough.

"Okay, okay. I get the picture. So how do I defeat an evil this intense?"

"Answer is unknown at this time."

"Well, do you have any suggestions?"

"Perhaps. Please be advised, this is an untested hypothesis...."

"What?"

"Perhaps you could counteract Number 1's negative force with slightly more than an equal measure of positive energy."

"Really? Fight evil with good? That's all you've got?"

"It is a notion worthy of your thoughtful consideration. By tipping the balance in the universal duality between good and evil, you may be able to overwhelm Number 1 and eliminate his threat to this galaxy."

Duality.

There was that word again.

The same one the strange girl on the train had called *a fascinating concept. One that might be good for you to remember.*

Chapter 32

NOW THE TUSK computer's panels glowed an orange red.

"This is the color of the Legions of the Light," the computer reported. "The color of confidence and creative power. *Your* color."

"Who are the Legions of the Light?" I asked.

"Those who bravely battle against Zeboul, the forces of darkness. The Legions of the Light are bathed in the warmth of the sun."

"Okay," I said, eager for a little backup of my own, "where exactly are these warm and glowing legions? I could definitely use an army right about now."

"Wherever you find negative energy you will also find its positive opposite. The two must always be in balance for the universe to maintain its equilibrium. This duality explains how you could come from Alpar Nok to protect the universe while others could come from the same planet to destroy it."

"And Number 1 is trying to tip the scales, once and for all, toward Zeboul and darkness?"

"Such is the hypothesis."

In other words, the computer didn't really know.

"But," the mechanical voice continued, "The Light is powerful. For centuries, it has inspired the Alien Hunters of the Alpar Nokian Protectorship. It has moved earthlings, such as Bahā' Allāh, Mahatma Gandhi, and Abraham Lincoln to seek out the better sides of human nature. It is the force that will communicate to you through Xanthos and Mikaela, your spiritual advisors."

Wait, Mikaela was my spiritual advisor, too? I nodded, soaking it all in.

"May I help you with anything else at this time, Graff?" asked the computer.

"No," I said, without telling the thing I wasn't my dad. "Thanks."

I sat there for a moment, staring at the Tusk computer, which, having answered my questions, had flipped back to televising twelve different kinds of soccer being played on planets scattered across the universe.

"You remind me so much of your father," said a gentle female voice behind me.

I turned around.

It was Mikaela. The girl from the train. And the one who would help me save the world.

Chapter 33

MIKAELA LOOKED COMPLETELY different.

For one thing, she wasn't wearing glasses or a short skirt. Instead, she had on a loose-fitting karategi tied with a bright red belt, which, by the way, is even higher than a black belt in many martial arts. I noticed that the pants and top of her white karate uniform were done in the kata cut-style, the design choice for elite competitors. She was also bathed in a warm incandescent glow that followed her every move as if she were being tracked by a sunbeam.

Mikaela was definitely playing for the Legions of the Light, just like Xanthos, who carried the same kind of golden aura when he galloped across that open pasture back at the Judges' ranch.

"So, Mikaela," I said, folding down the Tusk and tucking it my pocket, "I take it you're not really a teenager?"

She smiled. "Only when I need to be."

I couldn't tell you exactly how old she was, but even though her face was as smooth and creamy as an infant's,

I had a feeling her soul was as old as that meteorite back at the American Museum of Natural History.

"Just out of curiosity," I said, "did you get off the train in Philly or Baltimore?"

She grinned. "Somewhere in between."

"And you were my father's *backup* spiritual advisor?"

"I like to think that Xanthos and I worked together as a team to aid Graff in his work as a torchbearer and protector of all that is good. In the same way, I would like to assist you, Daniel. Your reactions in fight-or-flight situations intrigue me. They intrigue all those who dwell in the light."

"How so?"

"Your choices, much like your father's, seldom make logical or analytical sense."

I couldn't disagree. I guess a lot of what we Alien Hunters do is totally illogical. Going up against alien creeps and their minions when we're hopelessly outnumbered. Turning into flies, cockroaches, or household appliances just so we can stay in the game. Giving up any shot at a normal life so we can protect the lives of others.

Okay, you could even call us crazy.

"Where is the nearest clustering of human creatures?" Mikaela asked.

"Excuse me?"

"Where is the closest earthling population center?"

I shrugged. "Stafford, I guess. It's a small town about twelve miles southwest of here. Why?"

Mikaela didn't answer. She just nodded knowingly.

That's when the sky began to darken into a greenish-black swirl of angry thunderheads.

The low-hanging clouds started to rotate. Dust and debris whirled on the ground as a sudden torrent of rain pelted us. But just as quickly as it had started the rain stopped, leaving a dead calm.

And then I heard the roar and rumble of a jet-powered freight train tearing across the sky.

A monstrous funnel cloud appeared on the horizon, its tail dipping down to churn up the earth.

It was a twister; a tornado headed south-by-southwest.

Heading straight for Stafford, Kansas.

Chapter 34

THE TWISTER WAS roaring down the long-abandoned Union Pacific railroad tracks, its sights set on the 1,344 friendly people who called Stafford, Kansas, their home.

I remembered visiting Stafford, a nearby town, once when I was a toddler.

My mother and father took me to a restaurant called the Curtis Café, famous for its handwritten menu, home-made pies, and completed jigsaw puzzles lining all the wood-paneled walls.

If I didn't stop this tornado, every one of those puzzles would be torn back into its thousands of pieces again. So would every building on Main Street.

Furious, I glanced over at Mikaela, who had clearly called up the life-threatening twister. She had a way-too-angelic expression on her face for someone who wasn't exactly acting on the side of good so far.

In fact, she looked like she was studying me. Waiting

for my reaction to the crisis. I guess I was her little white lab rat. Would I fight the tornado or would I flee the scene?

The basement of my old house doubled as a storm cellar, so that would've been the logical choice.

Hide down there. Ride out the storm.

But they had really, *really* good raisin cream pie at the Curtis Café down in Stafford.

"I'll be back," I promised my strange visitor, who was still bathed in her warm glow even though the sky above us looked like soggy balls of sooty cotton.

Fueled by the surging need to protect others, my powers felt like they had been ratcheted up to a mathematically impossible one-hundred-and-ten percent. Making like a champion figure skater, I went up on one toe, held up both arms, and applied force to generate torque on my axis of rotation. When my angular momentum had me spinning, I brought down my arms to reduce my moment of inertia and increase my angular velocity.

Twirling dizzily, faster than Natalia Kanounnikova when she set the Guinness ice spinning record of 308 revolutions per minute, I rearranged my molecular structure so I became a whirling dervish of a dust cloud. After centrifugal force had expanded me outward to the size of an Arabian dust storm, I tore across the flat plains and became the first tornado ever to chase a tornado.

Seconds later, I smacked my whirlwind self into the cyclone Mikaela had whipped up and became one with the twister heading for Stafford. Through the power of my imagination, our gale-force winds merged and we became a single gigantic funnel cloud full of dust, death, and destruction. The instant the first tornado's molecular structure became grafted onto mine, I took over as cyclone pilot and set a new course: straight up into the sky.

In a flash, we weren't in Kansas anymore.

We were about thirty thousand feet above it, and above all those angry clouds.

Chapter 35

I DIDN'T STOP spinning my funnel cloud until I reached the frozen edge of the mesosphere, about fifty-three miles above ground.

Weather balloons and jet aircraft can't reach this layer of the atmosphere. Rockets pass through on their way up to their orbits but they don't hang out. I was totally alone.

I became myself for a nanosecond as I released the kinetic energy of the whirlwind. The dust particles instantly turned to ice because the temperature at the ceiling of the mesosphere was a very brisk *minus* 130 degrees. Up here, the air is so thin that the atoms and molecules of gases hardly ever bump into each other.

To warm myself, I morphed into a flaming meteorite. The mesosphere is where meteorites turn into shooting stars. So, blazing a brilliant comet tail, I scorched across the sky and hoped somebody down on Earth was making a wish on me.

I know what I would've wished for: Number 1 turning into a big fat zero.

When I had plummeted to a safe altitude of thirty thousand feet (well, safe for me, but please don't try this the next time the pilot says you've reached your final cruising altitude), I transformed out of a comet into just your average teenager in full HAHO (High Altitude High Opening) jump gear. HAHO parachute jumps are sometimes used for the covert insertion of Special Forces personnel, like my friend, the Navy SEAL, into enemy territory. You pop open your chute about four miles higher than a weekend jumper would.

When I hit twenty-seven thousand feet (I could see a Delta flight about one hundred miles north at the same altitude) I pulled the rip cord to deploy my parachute.

Only it didn't open.

Nothing popped out of the High Altitude Precision Parachute System I had whipped up for my trip home. As my rate of descent increased, my cheeks and the high tech fabric in my jump suit were flapping like flags in a hurricane.

But I didn't panic.

I had altitude, which meant I had time.

Maybe I could turn myself into a hawk or an eagle and swoop to safety.

It sounded like a plan.

Only it didn't work.

I don't know if it was the thin air and all those molecules and atoms not bumping into each other that was throwing off my molecular rearrangement capabilities. Or maybe I hadn't given myself sufficient time to recover from the mental strain of turning myself into a tornado. Whatever the reason, I knew I couldn't pull off the major metamorphosis I needed before I ended up like Wile E. Coyote at the bottom of a canyon.

Fortunately, I also knew I would soon reach my terminal velocity—the point where a free-falling body (me) stops picking up speed because the downward pull of gravity equals the upward force of drag, resulting in an acceleration factor of zero.

Unfortunately, the speed I would be falling when I hit my terminal velocity would also be "terminal" (as in deadly) when I smacked into the ground.

So I tugged at the ripcord again.

And again.

Nothing.

My incredible imagination had done an incredibly lousy job packing my main chute. I was spinning and twisting and spiraling out of control.

Heading straight for death at 200 miles per hour.

Chapter 36

AS THE GROUND rushed up to meet me and the blistering air gushed past my ears, my father's words echoed in my head: *Remember, son, you must always have a backup. It isn't a weakness to be prepared. It is a strength.*

Or, as they say in skydiving circles, "When in doubt, whip the second one out."

When I passed through two thousand feet, I yanked on the reserve rip cord.

KABOOM!

My backup parachute exploded out of the nylon pack strapped across my chest.

The rainbow-colored fabric deployed in a perfectly ruffled arc over my head and was yanked up into the sky like a wild animal caught in a snare trap. Then I started drifting downward. Slowly.

I could see my old house.

I could see Mikaela waiting for me in the backyard.

And, best of all, I could see the town of Stafford safe in the distance.

When my feet finally touched ground, I used the forward momentum of my landing to trot right over to Mikaela, hoping I would slam into her *accidentally*, but no such luck.

"You did extremely well, Daniel," she said serenely.

I chuffed an ugly laugh. "Not really. I would've ended up flatter than a Taco Bell tostada if I hadn't had backup, no thanks to you." She said nothing as I unhooked my parachute gear. "So, was that some kind of test?"

"Yes," answered Mikaela.

"Well, not to tell you how to do your job," I said, as I cut free my chute lines, "but the next time you whip up a little pop quiz, try not to endanger the lives of 1,344 innocent civilians."

Sunset colors lit up the horizon. There wasn't a single cloud in the sky, angry or otherwise, just a sparkling display of stars emerging. My time was running out.

"The people of Stafford were never in danger," Mikaela said gently. "If you had chosen to flee to the storm cellar and hide, I would have terminated the tornado. But, Daniel? This test was nothing compared to what The Prayer will soon put you through."

"Really? Well, thanks for the practice run. If Number 1 sends a tornado, cyclone, typhoon, or water funnel at me, I guess I'll know how to handle it."

"A meteorological catastrophe is nothing compared to the weapons The Prayer has at its disposal."

"You mean the Opus 24/24?"

Mikaela shook her head. "Something worse."

"I don't care," I said. "That thing, that force of darkness, IT killed my parents. Taking down Number 1 has been my sole purpose on Earth for over a decade."

"Even though the smart choice would be to walk away, journey to a distant, untroubled planet and live another day?"

"Hey, what good is living if a monster is killing everybody and everything you ever loved?"

"I am impressed, Daniel. Not many would embrace the path you have chosen. In fact, your irrational, emotional choices seem to violate the very essence of what being an 'intelligent' life form means."

"So call me stupid," I said with a shrug. "It's who I am. It's who my mother and father raised me to be. Blame them. Hey, blame yourself. After all, you were my dad's spiritual advisor. Maybe you planted some of this unintelligent behavior in his head and he just passed it on to me."

"Perhaps," Mikaela said with a smile. "And, for the record, we do not think you are stupid. In fact, we find you to be heroic."

"Well, I guess there's a fine line between heroism and stupidity, huh?"

"Be that as it may," said Mikaela, "we are intrigued and impressed with your actions. We will be watching."

"How many of you are there?"

"Enough, I hope. Continue to live dangerously, Daniel X. It may be your safest course of action."

And then the angelic girl I knew as Mikaela dissolved into a throbbing ball of orange-red light and shot up into the sky. She soared far beyond the mesosphere, past the thermosphere, out into the infinite reaches of space. She took her place among the twinkling stars in the sprawling constellation of Hercules, just west of Lyra, 27.4 light years away from Earth.

Hercules.

It's where we get the word "hero."

Chapter 37

EXHAUSTED (WHY DON'T *you* trying being a tornado, a comet, and a freaked-out free faller all in the same day?), I materialized a small tent and sleeping bag in the backyard of my former home.

I did *not* want to sleep inside the building where both my parents had been brutally slain. Nightmares—in IMAX 3-D with THX surround sound—would be guaranteed.

It took me a long time to drift off, even though I knew I needed the rest, especially if I wanted my parachute (or anything else) to work the next time I materialized one.

But I couldn't stop thinking about Mel.

Where had Number 1 taken her? Was she safe? Did she know that she shared her soul with Dana, my childhood friend?

That last question was so mind-numbingly metaphysical that I finally drifted off to sleep wrestling with it.

A sleep that didn't last long.

The ground shook. My eyes popped open. Something

enormous had just crash-landed in the backyard. Whatever it was, it had brought with it a darker kind of light than the golden aura of Mikaela and Xanthos. The walls of my tent were glowing under the influence of ultraviolet black-light radiation. My white socks and shoelaces looked like fluorescent ghosts.

I climbed out of my sleeping bag, yanked open the tent flaps, stumbled into the yard, and was face-to-face with my worst nightmare.

The six-and-a-half-foot-tall praying mantis monster stood in a hazy beam of black light. Make that a "preying" mantis, because the thing was rubbing its spiked forelegs together, eager for its next kill.

"Hello, Danny Boy," it boomed in its deep voice. "The hero returns to his pathetic little hovel in Kansas. I appreciate the poetry of your choice. So many of your family members have died in this spot. It is right that *you* should die here, too."

The foul beast sprang one giant leap forward on its massively muscled legs—covering fifteen feet in a single hop. Its grossly bulging, plum-colored body jiggled when it landed right in front of me.

"You silly little fool," it hissed through its jagged, glass-shard teeth. Its breath reeked with the scent of maggot-riddled beef rotting in the sun. "Wasting precious time entertaining my boring, oversentimental cousin, Mikaela? Riding around with that ridiculous Pfeerdian freak, Xanthos?"

I couldn't resist taunting the beast.

"You mean the Legions of the Light? The two golden oldies that terrify you?"

"I fear *NOTHING*!" The Prayer screeched, rearing back its tiny triangular head on its stalk of a neck. "I feed on fear. And you, Daniel, have much to be afraid of."

"I am afraid." I stepped back a foot or two, fanning the air in front of my face. "Of that rancid butcher shop you call your breath."

"Foolish child. You should have spent this day seeking out a good hiding place on a distant planet, far removed from the gravitational pull of my ever-expanding black hole."

"Are we talking about your mouth again?" I shot back. "Because you should really see an orthodontist about those broken-bottle teeth of yours. Maybe get yourself fitted for a retainer."

The Prayer didn't like me snapping on his crooked excuses for teeth.

I heard a gurgling, mucusy, wet sound. But instead of hocking a loogie at me, the thing shot a gelatinous glob of blue flame out of his wide-open pie hole.

I dodged the fireball and zipped to my right, making sure I had a tree between the fire-spewing wackaloon and me.

"You cannot hide!" The Prayer bellowed. "There is no planet, no dimension, no space or time where I cannot find you."

The Prayer hopped forward and, grabbing a clump of branches with both its pincers, wrenched my tree—roots and all—right out of the ground.

Tossing the tree aside as if it were a twig, Number 1 glared down at me with its liquid-black bug eyes.

"Say good-bye to Terra Firma, Daniel. Your days as the Alien Hunter end here. They end *now*!"

Chapter 38

I PRAYED MIKAELA wasn't watching from her heavenly perch.

Because, presented with my next fight-or-flight choice, I went with option B.

As in, *run away.*

And, in case you're keeping score, I've gotten much better at teleporting near the clutches of an alien outlaw, even the top dog.

I caught a glimpse of The Prayer grasping at me with his pincers but, when the claws clamped shut, there was nothing for him to rip to shreds.

I was already in Florida. St. Pete Beach.

Why did I pick the gulf coast of the Florida peninsula? I thought Disney World would be too crowded. Other than that, I just wanted to be someplace warm and sunny for a couple of minutes.

Unfortunately, my vacation in the Sunshine State was cut short when The Prayer emerged out of the foamy surf and hopped across the sand—scattering beachgoers, trampling sun umbrellas, stomping on sand castles.

So I let my mind go limp and dove below the surface of time.

I went back to my train ride from New York to D.C. I knew The Prayer hadn't been there, probably because it was afraid of Mikaela. I figured he'd stay away if I went back.

"Would you like a Sprite, Daniel?" Mikaela asked me (again).

"Um, no."

"I would. Excuse me. I'm going to the café car." She stuffed her book back into her knapsack.

It was time to slightly alter the past and stick with Mikaela. I was hoping she could be my guardian angel and protect me from The Prayer just long enough for me to figure out how to make the beast yearn for *its* guardian devil.

"Hey, maybe I should go with you," I said. "I hear Amtrak has the best hot dogs in the world, maybe the universe."

"Fine," said Mikaela.

Only it wasn't her.

How could I tell? The last time we were together, Mikaela's breath didn't stink of rotting flesh or moldy cheese.

I was out of that train car before The Prayer had morphed out of his college-girl-with-glasses disguise—something I was extremely glad about because I did *not* want to see those gangly legs in a miniskirt.

I zoomed back to Kentucky.

The horse barn.

I remembered how The Prayer had reacted when Xanthos came charging across the field at him.

"NO!" it had shrieked. "Keep away! I have claimed this one for the darkness!" And then Number 1 had spewed its blue jelly fireballs, but Xanthos did not back down.

Because Xanthos's light canceled out The Prayer's darkness. They were polar opposites. Hot and cold, love and hate, yin and yang. The Prayer could not destroy Xanthos. Similarly, Xanthos could not destroy The Prayer.

That was *my* job.

I raced into the horse barn. "Xanthos?" I called as I rushed over to his stall.

No answer.

"My brudda?" I shouted as I braced the bars of his cozy pen to see if he was sleeping.

It was empty.

But there was movement in the dark shadows at the far corner of the stall. Xanthos!

Nope.

"You miserable little brat," brayed The Prayer as it crept out of the gloom. Its right pincer was gripping the same Opus 24/24 with the charred muzzle that he had used to murder my parents years ago.

"You're the best that the Alpar Nokian Protectorship can find to go up against a being as mighty as ME? I possess all the dark powers and the Legions of the Light put their hope and trust in YOU?" It laughed mirthlessly. "You are a gutless coward, an infant crawling here and there, spending more than ten Earth years HIDING from the confrontation you've always known would be your last. Your weakness sickens me, Danny Boy. You are the same insignificant brat you were when you hid in that basement and used silly trickery to save your own life instead of bravely avenging your parents' deaths! You were a coward then, and you are a coward now."

I'd heard enough.

I stepped forward.

I was about to introduce the alien freak to the deadlier examples of my "silly trickery" when—*BAM*!

The thing swung its left arm out of the murky gloom.

And I saw its other weapon.

Mel.

Chapter 39

"DANIEL?" GASPED MEL. "Where have you been? Why didn't you come for me?"

"Because," said The Prayer, chuckling, "your so-called soul mate has been too busy running away from me and playing superhero with a pretty thing named Mikaela."

"That's not true," I said, sounding way too defensive.

""Why didn't you rescue me, Daniel?" cried Mel, sounding a whole lot needier than she ever had before. Even her brilliant blue eyes looked weak and watery.

I remembered what Xanthos had communicated to me the day I first set eyes on Melody Judge: *Her name is Mel, short for Melody, a name that suits her personality quite well, yah? She is like the song you hear in the morning and cannot get out of your head all day.* Mel was an incredibly brave girl, normally, but being The Prayer's prisoner had clearly traumatized her. Seeing her this way made me even angrier.

"Did that thing hurt you?" I asked.

"Not yet," she choked out. "Help me, Daniel. Save me."

"Don't worry," I said, hoping to crack through her thick veneer of fear. "If this creepazoid even looks at you the wrong way, I'll braid his stupid dreadlocks together into ponytails so he looks like the Swiss Miss girl on a carton of pudding cups."

Mel didn't smile. The Prayer jostled her forward.

"Take your stinking paws off her, you dirty insect!" I yelled. "Leave Mel out of this."

"With pleasure, Daniel. All you have to do is agree to my previous terms."

"Daniel?" said Mel, her voice panicky, sounding like the opposite of her spunky self. "What's Number 1 talking about?"

I tried to play it off. "Nothing."

"NOTHING?" shrieked The Prayer. "It is *EVERYTHING*!"

The giant mantis stomped its feet like a long-legged three-year-old throwing a temper tantrum.

"Daniel?" Mel was whimpering, her body trembling.

I moved toward her.

"NO!" roared The Prayer, hopping between us. "You cannot touch her until you agree to my terms. You are Number One on my list, *Danny Boy*. Make the exchange now or I will withdraw my very generous offer!"

I had to get Mel safely away from this insane insectoid.

That was step one.

Step two would be kicking the big bug's butt. Because if I didn't, Melody Judge and every other human being currently inhabiting planet Earth would soon be sucked into a death spiral of oblivion, courtesy of Number 1's fast-growing black hole.

"Okay," I said. "You've got a deal. No more tricks. No more leaps across time or space. You can kill me, right after you set Mel free."

Chapter 40

"EXCELLENT!" CHORTLED THE Prayer. "Kiss your girlfriend good-bye, Daniel. It is time for you to join your mother, your father, and all your young Alpar Nokian friends on the far side of life."

Much to my surprise, The Prayer retreated two giant steps, giving Mel and me a little privacy to say our good-byes.

I took hold of Mel's shoulders with both my hands and sidled around so all Number 1 could see was my back.

"Don't worry," I whispered. "As soon as you're safe, I'm going to bring that thing a whole galaxy of hurt."

Mel didn't smile. Or offer to fight Number 1 with me. She didn't even try to talk me out of exchanging my life for hers.

Instead, she stared at me with vacant, ice-blue eyes.

"Are you okay?" I asked. "Did that thing drug you? Did it get inside your head?"

I thought about all the brainwashing and memory

scrubbing I've done in my time as the Alien Hunter. Surely the Number 1 evil alien of the twenty-first century could do the same.

"Mel?" I said loudly, in case she'd gone deaf. "Are you in there? This is me. Daniel."

Finally, she spoke. "I know who you are, Daniel."

Her stone-cold blue eyes filled with red-hot rage. She was staring at me with nothing but dark, undiluted hatred.

I moved in to hug her, hoping that the warmth of my body would melt away whatever deep freeze of a trance Number 1 had zapped into the girl of my dreams.

That's when the nightmare began.

Mel dropped down and lunged forward, locking her hands behind my knees and executing a perfect double-leg takedown. I hit the ground hard. But, fighting my body's natural instinct to tense up when attacked, I didn't let my knees lock. Instead, I went with her momentum, kept my knees bent, and rolled her forward over my head.

When I twisted over and sprang to my feet, Mel was already coming toward me at a run. She leaped up, raised her knee, then snapped her foot forward in a powerful front kick to my face.

I took the blow and landed flat on my back.

Mel pounced on my chest, pinning me down with her knees.

"Okay," I gasped. "I think we need to have a serious talk."

"Fine," she said, linking her hands together, raising them over her head, and bringing her double fist down like a pile driver to my mouth. My mouth filled with blood and a couple of teeth went a little loose in my jaw. "Talk through that."

"Enough," I gurgled, holding up both my hands to beg for a momentary ceasefire—mostly because I didn't want to hurt her (or lose any teeth).

Mel bounded up off my chest and laughed.

I sat up and spat out the blood.

"What did that thing do to you?" I asked. Was she an imposter? It didn't seem like it—she even had the faint scar that I wasn't able to heal, despite my best efforts.

Mel was grinning like a lunatic.

"Nothing compared to what we're about to do to *you*," she said. Then she gracefully twirled around and donkey-kicked me right between the eyes.

That's when my whole world went dark.

Chapter 41

WHEN I WOKE UP, I was strapped to a stainless steel table with gutters running down its edges to a drain hole.

The Prayer was leaning over the table, hungrily rubbing its jagged forelegs together in anticipation of a feast. Its bulbous black eyes, glistening like oil-slicked basketballs, were maybe six inches away from my face. Its snakeskin snout twitched as its red dreadlocks dribbled down between its antennae to tickle my chest and neck.

I fought against my restraints but it was no use. I was trapped like a formaldehyded frog pinned to a block of wax.

I glanced to my left.

Mel was holding a pair of jumper cables.

"Call it the Stockholm syndrome," Number 1 boasted. "The kidnap victim now sides with her captor...ME! But, can you blame her, Danny Boy? You see, I showed Melody a little snippet of you and Dana sleeping under the stars in that worthless museum. I showed her how you

151

were gawking at that stardust girl when she sashayed onto your train. Poor, poor little orphan boy Danny. You had no father to teach you about girls because I *killed* him before he could. So, allow *me* to school you: Hell hath no fury like a woman scorned!"

"Wait a second...." I zeroed in on Mel. "You *are* Dana. Dana is you...."

But she wasn't listening.

She was clamping her jumper cables to my toes. One was the grounding cable. The other a hot-wire.

She flicked a switch and sent a sizzling electrical shock soaring through my neuromuscular system. The pain was excruciating.

And then it stopped. I nearly cried from relief.

Until Mel hit the switch for the second time.

My body spasmed. My fingers splayed out in agony. My back bucked and my head banged against the hard steel table.

That's when I knew the girl torturing me wasn't Mel.

Melody Judge could never be that cruel to any living creature.

Clearly, this torture was going on inside my head, though the burns on my wrists from straining against the straps felt pretty real.

The Mel thing flicked the switch again, cutting off the electricity that had fried who knows how many of my brain's synapses—right when I needed my full mental powers. If this torture was a mind game, the only way to fight back would be to imagine the pain away.

But before I could, the Mel thing flipped the switch again.

"No," I begged through numb lips as my body convulsed on the table. "Stop. Please."

The Prayer mocked my pleading. "*S-s-top! P-p-p-lease!* Ha!"

So did the thing that wasn't really Mel. "What a wuss!"

Then she cranked up the voltage.

I knew the pain searing every fiber of my being wasn't real but it seemed a whole lot worse than real.

I couldn't take it anymore.

"Mel!" I screamed hysterically. "Whoever you are. Stop. Please!"

All I heard in response to my plea was uncontrollable laughter.

From The Prayer and his newest disciple: my soul mate Mel.

Chapter 42

WRITHING IN AGONY on that cold stainless steel table, my girlfriend's merry giggles torturing me mentally as the electricity shattered me physically, I have never, *ever* felt so broken.

The twisted avatar of Mel was killing me with pain.

I was a total disgrace. Weak. Unable to defend myself, let alone a whole planet. Worst of all, I had dishonored my parents' missions on Earth and their memories by letting their killer escape justice for so long. And now that the horrid creature had me in its clutches. I had no hope of avenging them.

On the humiliation scale of one to ten, I was somewhere near thirty.

This was worse than that dream I sometimes have of showing up naked at school. A school where all the teachers are nuns.

Worse than finally summoning up the courage to call

up a cute girl to ask her out and hearing nothing but laughter in reply.

For the first time ever, I wished I was dead.

I was done. Whatever mind games The Prayer was playing with me, they were working brilliantly.

I was ready to call it quits.

I was about to beg the horrid insect to slice through my neck with a quick snap of its saw-toothed claws, hoping the instant I became "the late Daniel X," the pain, shame, and embarrassment would stop.

And then, in a blink of an eye, the pain went away.

Had my fervent wish come true? Was I dead?

No.

I was still lying on the cold steel table. The Prayer was still hovering over me.

Mel was gone.

"*OUT!*" The Prayer screeched triumphantly.

"Wha-a-a?" I mumbled.

"Out! Go! Run away, Danny Boy."

I raised one arm and then the other. The straps binding me to the surgical table had been removed. I was able to sit up. I swiveled around to face the beast.

"Why didn't you finish this?" I spat out weakly.

"*Finish* it? No, no, no. This cannot end so easily, Danny Boy. You are being released so I may have the sublime pleasure of hunting you down yet again." Its scaly snout twitched rapidly. "Catch, torture, and release, Daniel. Catch, torture, and release. I *so* look forward to doing all of this again! You are the last of my targets. The top name on my list. We must allow your exquisite pain and my delicious pleasure to go on and on and on. We *cannot* end our splendid story so soon, can we? Where's the sport in that?"

The Prayer rocked back its head, rolled it around on its stick of a neck, and laughed fiendishly.

"Go!" it commanded. "Do what your dead daddy told you to do. Go find your 'backup.' And, when you find it, bring it *back* to me!"

The beast exhaled a blast of putrid sewer gas at me. The reeking stench made me grimace and recoil.

I *so* wanted to fight back.

To take down The Prayer, right then and there.

I was through playing games. I was also done with self-pity and wishing I were dead. Now I had a different kind of death wish: for this giant, gangly, murdering monster to finally pay the price for what it had done to my family; for what it had just done to me on its torture table.

But I couldn't.

It was like I was drugged again. That misty blast of green puke gas from Number 1's quivering schnozzle must've been some kind of nerve gas or knockout powder.

My eyelids felt like they were tethered to dumbbells.

I toppled back on the table. All I could do was close my eyes and sleep.

A very deep and dreamless sleep.

Chapter 43

I FINALLY WOKE UP. Totally frustrated and beyond confused.

Because I was in a bed. A hospital bed.

The same hospital bed I had woken up in before. I recognized the blue knit blanket.

A nurse dressed in scrubs with a stethoscope draped around her neck leaned into my field of vision.

"I'm Nurse O'Hara," she said with a smile. "It's so good to see your beautiful blue eyes, Daniel."

It was her again.

"Where am I?"

"The hospital. Intensive care."

I tried to sit up.

"Now, now. You mustn't push yourself, Danny Boy."

Danny Boy. This time, I knew for sure where "Nurse O'Hara" picked up that little pet name. The Prayer. This was probably the start of my next torture round in the twisted "catch, torture, and release" hunting game.

"Saints be praised!" crowed the way-too-Irish nurse. "You're alive."

I shook my head in disbelief and smirked. "This is the part where the three doctors come in, right?"

Nurse O'Hara looked momentarily puzzled by that.

"Yep," I said, as three white coats strode into the room. "Right on cue."

"Good morning, Daniel," chirped the handsome guy with perfect hair who looked like he'd just waltzed off the set of that TV show *The Doctors*.

"We heard the good news," said the one who looked like Dr. Sanjay Gupta.

"It's a miracle," said Nurse O'Hara, wiping a fake tear from her rosy cheek. The second time through, she was definitely overplaying it. Going borderline Soap Opera on me.

I knew this whole scene was another move in The Prayer's Olympic-sized mind games. This was the ultimate torture: taking me out of commission while the forces of darkness's solar-system-sucking black hole grew and grew like a giant zit on the tip of the Milky Way's nose. Number 1 was buying time for Terra Firma to reach its event horizon—that point of no return.

"So," I said, "I guess I had a motorcycle accident?"

"That's right," said Dr. Gupta. "It's a very encouraging sign that you remember what happened, Daniel."

I shrugged. "Whatever. I've been in another coma, huh?"

"Another?" asked one more familiar-looking doctor.

"What was I gone for this time? *Eighteen* months? Two years? Or did I totally Rip Van Winkle it this time and now it's like twenty years in the future and earthlings are buzzing around with jetpacks on their backs?"

All three doctors and the nurse were gawking at me like I was insane.

"You know the funny thing about comas?" I said. "No matter how many you guys tell me I've had or how long I've been conked out, I never seem to age at all."

"Daniel," said the Dr. Gupta look-alike. "You need to rest."

"You'd like that, wouldn't you?" I said, looking up to the ceiling, figuring Number 1 was somewhere watching this daytime drama unfold.

I tossed off my hospital blanket and yanked aside the sheets.

"You're not to leave that bed, young man," scolded Nurse O'Hara.

"Or what? You guys will haul in another set of jumper cables and a couple of car batteries? Or maybe this time, since the hospital bed is adjustable, you'll just tilt it back and waterboard me."

Nurse O'Hara turned to the handsome dude. "Dr. Fabricius? Do something!"

The doc reached into the deep hip pocket of his lab coat.

Before he could extract another syringe filled with blackout serum, I sprang out of the bed, spun around, and landed a roundhouse kick to the handsome man's breadbasket. He clutched his stomach, dropped to his knees, and tried to remember how to breathe.

I went for Dr. Gupta next.

He was coming at me with a wickedly sharp needle. I swung up my arm and locked my hand around his wrist, catching him in midthrust.

Then, twisting his wrist until I heard it pop, I brought that needle down hard and gave the good doctor a taste of his own medicine—right in the thigh. Dr. Gupta's eyes rolled back in their sockets as he drifted off to happy comaland.

Unfortunately, while I was administering my treatment to Dr. Gupta, I felt a needle jab in my butt.

I glanced over my shoulder.

Nurse O'Hara.

She was smiling at me and holding up a shimmering syringe. Her smile wasn't the friendly sort, either; it was more like a "we'll see who's in charge here, young man" kind of smirk.

As the sedative swam through my bloodstream and my brain began to fog, all I could hear was my father's voice calling out to me from somewhere far, far away:

Go look for your backup, son! Find your backup!

Chapter 44

BUT *WHAT* WAS my backup?

Where was my backup?

I became totally obsessed with trying to decipher my father's cryptic message.

Is there some weapon I'm supposed to find? Some ally? Maybe another warrior to help me take down The Prayer?

I was so fixated on figuring out what it was my father wanted me to do that I started muttering my internal monologue out loud.

"Who's my backup? Where's my backup?"

Was I going crazy?

The so-called doctors and nurses sure seemed to think so. They tied my arms and legs to the hospital bed with thick leather straps buckled tight.

"Find my backup? What's my backup? Should I back up the Tusk computer?"

When I started asking the scoop of mashed potatoes on my cafeteria tray these questions (over and over) the doctors decided to transfer me to the psychiatric wing of the hospital.

This time, when they rolled me down the halls, they were really halls and not just canvas flats from a Hollywood movie set. It was a *real* hospital. It even smelled like chicken broth mixed with antiseptic.

I realized: I might truly be insane. This whole Daniel X thing could be a figment of my imagination. All the running around in New York City, Kentucky, and Kansas could've taken place right here in a hospital bed—in my head!

Could this be my real reality? Was Daniel X just a fevered dream?

Every day, usually after a snack of pills in tiny paper cups, I had to go to group therapy.

"The last time we spoke, Daniel," said Dr. Loesser, the psychiatrist in the tweed coat who liked to stroke his goatee, "you exhibited a great deal of hostility." He formed another fingertip tent under his nose and waited patiently for me to respond.

"Well," I said, "maybe I am slightly hostile because, like I told you yesterday, The Prayer got my girlfriend, Mel, who is really Dana, to give me electroshock therapy with jumper cables hooked up to some kind of high voltage spaceship battery."

I was sitting on a plastic chair in a circle that included the psychiatrist and seven other patients. Half of them looked numbed out on drugs. The other half was drooling in anticipation, wondering what kind of kooky stuff I'd say next.

I did not disappoint.

"Maybe I should've stayed a cockroach," I said.

My fans in the group circle giggled.

"Pardon?" said the doctor, arching a single eyebrow.

"After I teleported to New York City to get away from all those giant Mack trucks that had turned into humongous bulldogs, I turned *myself* into a cockroach so I could escape the lightning bolts being hurled at me in the middle of Times Square."

Dr. Loesser stroked his beard some more. "I see. And how did that make you feel, Daniel?"

"Pretty small and insignificant at first. But then I found this puddle of spilled Coke. No bubbles, just sticky syrup. Yum."

"Daniel," the shrink started, "it seems..."

I held up my hand to stop him. "I know. You're going to tell me that when I had my motorcycle accident I ran over a cockroach and it had a lightning-bolt marking on its thorax."

"No," said Dr. Loesser. "I was going to say that, given your high level of anger and bitterness, it seems you have reached the alienation phase of coping with your trauma."

I nodded. "Makes sense. After all, I'm an alien here in your nation."

The *whole* group cracked up at that one. Even the zonked out zombies.

When I joined in and started laughing like a maniac, too, Dr. Loesser raised a single finger to summon an orderly.

Another linebacker in white came at me with another syringe filled with bye-bye juice.

The instant he jammed the needle into my arm, my head slumped forward. I drifted down into the spiraling black hole of unconsciousness again.

The last thing I heard was the group laughing at me.

And I may be wrong, but I think Dr. Loesser was laughing at me, too.

Chapter 45

WHEN I WOKE UP, I was back in my hospital bed.

"There he is!" said a supercheery voice that sounded like my mom, if my mom was being played by a cheesy sitcom actress. "I knew this would snap him out of it."

"We had to smuggle these in," she chirped, fanning her hand over an open foil container filled with a stack of piping hot pancakes. "But there's nothing like a hearty breakfast to cure whatever ails you, I've always said."

"And *I've* always said, 'Never argue with a boy's mother about what's best for him,'" joked a man who looked like my dad would've looked if my dad were ever on display in a wax museum. "So eat up, Daniel, those may be the last pancakes your mom ever makes."

"Huh?"

"Our pancake maker was stolen, *syruptitiously*. What a *waffle* experience."

Okay. Robo-Dad even cracked corny puns like my real

165

dad sometimes did. I had to applaud The Prayer's script-writing skills.

Either that, or I had gone completely bonkers.

"You're not insane, Daniel," said another mother who had materialized in my room. "These two are not who they claim to be."

"My puns aren't that lame," said a second father standing beside my mirror image mother. "Are they, Altrelda?"

"Sometimes, Graff," said Mom #2.

"Wait a second," said the first father. "Who the heck are Graff and Altrelda?"

"Those are Danny's made-up names for his space parents," said Mom #1. "But did space mom bring you your favorite food? Of course not. How could she? She's not real, Daniel."

The parents who called themselves Graff and Altrelda were both wearing silver elephant pendants, emblems of Alpar Nokian home-world solidarity. My real parental units received their pendants when they graduated from the Academy and accepted their first jobs in the Protectorship.

Or maybe I made all that up.

Maybe it was just another part of my imaginary, alternate reality.

"Eat these before they get cold, Daniel," said Mom #1. "I made them with chocolate chips and then sprinkled on powdered sugar."

"Hang on a sec," I said, turning to the other side of the bed and my other set of parents. "How can you guys even be here?"

"Easy," said my dad with the cocky grin I remember from our many hard-core training sessions. "Some part of your brain must have known you needed parental advice...."

"But, wait—you *can't* come back. I cast your souls to the wind. Remember, Mom? After Dad's spirit passed over, you said, 'None of us is immortal.' And then your spirit moved on, too."

My mother (or the one who seemed more like my mother than the other mother in the room) smiled. "It is true, Daniel. But those who lived their life in the light never truly die."

I looked to my dad; the one I felt *had* to be my dad.

He winked. "We love you, Daniel. *Always.*"

Okay. That nearly clinched it.

"We love you, Daniel. Always," had been my father's final words to me, right before he died.

But wait a second: The Prayer killed my father. The giant praying mantis monstrosity would've heard those words, too. This new set of parents could be another pair of pre-programmed imposters sent by Number 1 to mess with my head.

"Zeboul does not like this planet," said Dad #2. "Humanity, with its abundant reservoirs of goodness and light, is a constant irritant to the forces of darkness."

"Whoa," said Dad #1, "sounds like somebody in this room watches way too many *Star Wars* movies."

The other father didn't even react to that. "The next time Number 1 catches you, Daniel," he said with steely determination, "the thing will most certainly destroy you."

"And," added my other mother, "it will attempt to crush your soul to prevent it from moving on to the next realm. It will deny you access to the light and take you with it into the darkness."

I dropped my head into my pillow and closed my eyes tight.

Either I was an ordinary teenager named Daniel Manashil with a hyperactive imagination who had been in a bad motorcycle accident, or I was Daniel X, the earth's final protector.

If I was Daniel the Alien Hunter, then the fate of an entire solar system (not to mention the cosmic balance between good and evil) had come crashing down on my head.

If I was Daniel Manashil, I would have to erase all of this alternate universe crap from my mind once and for all, so I could go home, fix my motorcycle, and ask the Dana I knew from school to go with me to the homecoming dance.

Either way, I was definitely going to need some backup.

Too bad neither one of my dads had mentioned where I might find some.

PART THREE
FIGHTING FOR ETERNITY

Chapter 46

WHEN I OPENED my eyes, both sets of parents were still in the room.

Just then, a swath of violet-tinged light crept across the floor. I looked over to the door. The crack under it was a glowing strip of ultraviolet light.

"Mom!" I hollered. "Get down!"

The door burst open.

The Prayer had kicked it in with a quick blast from his muscular leg.

One set of parents—the mom and dad who had arrived first—quickly leaped back from the bed rails and huddled up against the wall, taking themselves out of harm's way.

The other set stood their ground.

(Quick footnote—if you're ever in a similar jam, here's how you can tell who your real parents are: they're the ones who don't abandon you in the face of danger.)

"*YOU!*" roared The Prayer in its deep, strangled voice. "I already killed you both!"

"You can't kill love," replied my mother extremely calmly, especially considering the fact that The Prayer was toting his sizzling Opus 24/24.

"Lower the gun, my friend," said my father.

"I am not your FRIEND! Die again, Alien Hunter!"

Once more, I heard a string of deafening explosions as Number 1 blasted my parents (or their spiritual essences or their ghosts or whatever had drifted back into my life) off to oblivion. It was like that night back in Kansas all over again. Only worse, because I didn't have any idea what happened to a blasted spiritual essence.

"Good shooting," said Fake Dad from the corner.

"I'll say," added Fake Mom.

"Ha! I am just getting started. That was nothing. Now it's time for the blood and guts and gore." I heard the whine of the Opus 24/24 recharging its pain resonator. "Game over, you pathetic little pukemeister!"

And he swung his weapon up and aimed it right at me.

Chapter 47

THIS COULD NOT be happening again!

But it was.

I quickly tucked, rolled, and hit the floor—putting the steel frame of the hospital bed between The Prayer and me.

I heard the crunch of the killing machine's triple-jointed feet as it tiptoed around the foot of the bed. "Come out, come out, wherever you are," it taunted.

Like that was going to happen.

I crawled underneath the bed to contemplate my options.

"He's under the bed, sir," said Fake Dad.

"Do you need a flashlight?" added ever-helpful Fake Mom. "I have one in my purse."

"*QUIET!*" screeched Number 1, sitting up on its rear and middle legs and wiggling its antennae to sniff the air the way a police dog sniffs suspicious suitcases. "I do not need your wretched illumination device. I can smell the boy. I can smell his FEAR."

This was just like that first time when I was a little kid. Me, hiding; Number 1 tracking me like the master predator it was.

Of course, I thought.

I had a plan that I knew would work because it had worked the first time I was in this same dilemma.

The Prayer dropped into a multiple-knee-creaking squat and swung its hideous head under the bed.

And found *absolutely nothing.*

Because I had just done what I did back in Kansas all those years ago. I made myself a little less conspicuous to the murderous monster by transforming myself into an Arthropoda Arachnida Acari Metastigmata. I had become a tiny tick, smaller than the period at the end of this sentence. A baby male dog tick, to be precise.

And I was giving The Prayer mad mantis disease because it couldn't find me.

"Not possible!" the frustrated freak gasped. "I smelled the boy under the bed a second ago!"

"He sort of disappeared," said the dorky dad.

"Poof!" added his cheery spouse.

While The Prayer contemplated evaporating my one-hundred-percent fake mom and dad, I was hit with a second inspiration.

Everybody always says, "The best offense is a good defense."

That meant the opposite must be true, too: "The best defense is a good offense."

The best way to protect myself from Number 1 was to attack him.

But not here. More importantly, not *now*.

So I did a quick, full-body mitosis. For those of you who've already forgotten everything that was on your biology final, that means I split all of my cells in half and became two ticks.

I sent both my tick bodies scurrying across the cold hospital floor, dodged around The Prayer's size fifty-nine feet, and scampered up the shoes and socks of Fake Mom and Fake Dad.

Then I threw open the palps at the sides of my mouthparts, pierced my phony parents' skins with my double chelicerae, and sank my barbed, needlelike hypostome into them.

That's right—I bit both their ankles and went vampire on them.

I started sucking their blood.

Chapter 48

LOCKED ON TO both my substitute parental units, I chose flight over fight once again—but only so I could stage the fight in my preferred arena.

I let my mind go limp and dove through the surface of time.

Since I had a solid grip on Fake Mom and Fake Dad—not to mention their blood mingling with mine—I was able to blast back to the past and drag the two of them with me.

My destination was Kansas, of course.

I was going back in time to that fateful day when The Prayer first entered my life. Back to when I was three years old, making the Seven Wonders of the Ancient World out of Play-Doh down in the basement.

At least, that's the time I was going to make Number 1 think I had traveled to.

In truth, I was only time-scrubbing to that day when The Prayer caught me camping in the backyard. I set my time arrival parameters on early evening, just before dinner. I would art-direct the scene to make sure it looked exactly like it had on that cursed night right before The Prayer slaughtered my entire family.

That's why I was bringing along a few props—specifically, body doubles for my mother and father. Physically, they had been good enough to almost fool me. Hopefully, they would be good enough to fool Number 1, too.

I assumed the "omnipotent" Prayer was time-diving right behind me. Any temporal jump I could make, I knew it could match.

I sensed, however, that the forces of darkness could be blinded by their single-minded devotion to cold and calculating logic. They weren't big on emotions like love (I had a feeling this is why they wanted to destroy Terra Firma and all the emotional earthlings inhabiting it). Creatures without a conscience or intuition—those driven only by the logical choices presented to them—are often the easiest to fool. Especially if you do something totally wacking nuts.

The Prayer would follow me down the time-warp rabbit hole because it would be a logical, predatory choice. It would not question where I was headed. The hunter would simply track its prey.

When Number 1 arrived in Kansas, I was pretty confident it would assume that I had gone back to that pivotal moment, right before both my parents were slain.

Something I've actually thought about doing at least a billion times since I mastered time travel.

Over and over, I've asked myself, *What if I could go back and stop Number 1 from doing what it did?*

What if I, the trained teenage Alien Hunter Daniel, could pop into our Kansas home two minutes before The Prayer showed up and, if nothing else, warn my parents that Number 1 was coming?

That would be so awesome, right?

Probably not.

Changing history has consequences. It'd be like chucking a cinder block into a calm lake. There'd be too many ripples rushing forward from that single impact point; enough turbulence to swamp the future and wash away tons of meaningful events.

For instance, all the good I had done during my dangerous days as the Alien Hunter might be undone. Several cities across the globe might be instantly wiped out by outlaw extraterrestrials because I wasn't there to stop them if I hadn't grown up an orphan, eager to take on my dead parents' missions. Worse, I may have only delayed the inevitable, and the next time The Prayer struck in the past, the fiend would take greater pains to kill me when it killed my parents.

In fact, if I stopped The Prayer from killing my parents, bizarre as it sounds, there was a slim possibility that I would vanish half a nanosecond later because of whatever happened in the tsunami of history being rewritten. I might already be dead in that alternate timeline.

Seriously: you don't want to mess with the past because

it will totally scramble your future and muddle what you call the present.

On the other hand, I was more than willing to mess with Number 1's mind, big-time.

Hey, he'd been doing it to me all along.

It was time to return the favor.

Chapter 49

I NEEDED TIME to set the stage.

The instant I arrived in Kansas, I morphed out of my double tick configuration back into my teenage self and enlisted another of my favorite powers: I slowed time down.

Okay—I practically froze it.

(This is also cool to do when engaged in something you never want to end such as drinking a chocolate milk shake.)

Using my imagination coupled with my photographic memory, I completely redecorated the house. I made it look exactly like it had looked when I was three years old—down to the throw rugs, overstuffed furniture, and framed old-world masterpieces hanging on the walls.

I propped up my pretend parents in the kitchen and living room, fighting the urge to pose Dummy Dad with his finger up his nose. I positioned Mom near the stove where she was stirring a simmering pot of her famous

Pork Chops Diablo, slow cooked in a spicy chili sauce with caramelized onions. I inherited my love for gourmet food from my mom, who could also whip up a mean chili dog.

More importantly, I wanted the kitchen to *smell* the way The Prayer remembered it smelling that night. The tantalizing scents of pork chops, chili powder, and perfectly cooked onions were definitely in the air.

Next, I imagined up a three-year-old me and placed him in the basement. I made sure the three-year-old Daniel lived up to my Alpar Nokian nickname of "Stinky Pants." I also popped open the lid on a couple of tubs of Play-Doh, so its salty-sweet kindergarten fragrance filled the air.

All these scents mingling in the air would definitely help sell the time and place. One huge thing I had picked up from studying The Prayer's battle tactics was its reliance on the sense of smell when stalking its prey.

I made one final check.

Everything looked and smelled as it had that night.

Now I had to focus on matching the sounds. I spent a few nanoseconds mentally projecting a script into the minds of the puppets The Prayer had fabricated to play its mind games on me.

When the dialogue was downloaded, I released my grip on time.

"Daniel?" said the mom look-alike. "Dinner will be ready in five minutes. Time to start wrapping things up, honey."

Using my ventriloquist skills, I pitched my voice higher and made it sound like it was coming up the steps from the cellar: "Yes, Mom. One minute. I'm making Play-Doh history down here."

"Of course you are, dear. I would expect nothing less. Love you. Always."

"Love you back, Mom. Always."

Yes, even when I was three years old I spoke like I'd already graduated college.

Time slipped forward.

I saw my mother humming as she stirred her stew pot. My dad was in his favorite chair, reading the local newspaper, lowering its crinkly sheets as he drifted off into a pre-dinner catnap.

I glanced at the wall clock hanging in the kitchen and mentally did the countdown. *Three, two, one...*

BOOM!

Right on cue, The Prayer crashed through the window and into the kitchen.

Showtime!

Chapter 50

"DON'T HURT US!" sobbed my make-believe mom, just as I programmed her to do. "Who are you?"

The Prayer, grinning devilishly, raised its pincer and froze time the same way I had frozen it.

We were definitely all even Steven in the powers department.

I saw its antennae twitch as it took in the smells of the kitchen and then the whole house.

The thing actually purred because it was so satisfied that it knew where (and, more importantly, *when*) it was.

Then, with a quick sideways flick of its cornstalk neck, The Prayer spied me spying him crashing into our mutual past.

"My, my, my, Danny Boy," sneered the sickening skee-void. "What an extremely logical choice. Flying back through time to our first, fateful day together? At long last, you show some small promise as an adversary."

"And you show your enormous stupidity," I sneered back. "Falling into my trap."

The giant mantis stalked around the room. I countered his every move. We were two deadly predators, circling each other.

"Clever, Danny Boy. Beat me here and you never become a poor little alien orphan. You never have to face all my many minions on The List. There is no hideous torture in your future. No black hole threatening to suck this putrid planet off into the vast void of space. Your choice of time for our final confrontation impresses me."

Psyche. My mind-trick trap was working.

"I'm so glad you approve," I said sarcastically, as I circled behind my stand-in dad who was frozen in midleap out of his chair. "I've been wanting to come back to this day my whole life. This is my chance at a do-over, Bug Face. If I kill *you* before you kill my parents, so much horrible history will change."

"So true," chortled Number 1, sliding to the left on his gangly limbs. "So true. Why, you could even save your pathetic planet if you killed me before I ordered its destruction. But of course, you couldn't."

I smiled. "You catch on quick. Especially for an insect with a brain the size of a frozen pea. Right here, right now, we'll erase all the pain you caused my family."

"*If,*" hissed The Prayer. "IF! A small but hugely important word, Danny Boy. *If* you can stop me before I do again what you were too cowardly to stop me from doing before."

"Hey," I said. "Cut me some slack. I was only three years old."

The beast rumbled up another contented purr. "For me, you will always be an infant, Danny Boy. What you suggest will never happen. *You* defeat ME? Ha! *NOT POSSIBLE!*"

"Never say never," I said confidently. "Besides, you've already messed up."

Confusion filled the giant insect's scuzzy black eyes.

"What?" It stamped its feet like a spoiled brat. *"HOW?"*

"Well, for one thing, you're making way too much noise," I said. "And, for another, you forgot to freeze time in the basement, thereby altering history."

A three-year-old me holding a ball of pink Play-Doh appeared at the top of the staircase leading down into the cellar.

I threw my voice over to my childhood self. "Mom? Dad? Who's this big loud bug?"

"Game over!" screamed The Prayer. "I will kill you now as I should have killed you then!"

In its blind rage, The Prayer stomped across the room, turning its back on the real me.

And giving me the chance I'd been waiting for all my life.

Chapter 51

SUMMONING UP EVERY ounce of my Level 3 strength, I flew across the room just as The Prayer went after mini-me with its saw-toothed forelegs.

"Leave the kid alone!" I shouted as I straddled the creep's back. I wrapped my legs around its thorax. I palmed both of its basketball-sized eyes with my hands.

Pushing down hard on the slimy orbs, I was attempting to crush the insect's skull in my vise grip—mostly because the thing was way too big for me to step on with my shoe.

But I forgot about the wings on its elongated abdomen.

The Prayer unfurled them in a flash and took off. Hanging on tight, I went along for the ride.

We tore through the ceiling of the living room, ripped through my old bedroom, crashed through another ceiling and the rolled-out fiberglass lining the attic floor. We splintered our way through the plywood and shingles of the roof, and hit the sky. Once we were outdoors and airborne, The Prayer reached back, behind its head, with its jagged forelegs. Using its superior strength (Level 11 beats Level 3 every time), it yanked me free of my double-eyeball grip and executed a series of flying barrel rolls to fling me off its back.

On my way down, I smashed new holes in the roof, the attic floor, and my bedroom's ceiling.

Fortunately, the cushy mattress in my old racecar bed broke my fall.

The Prayer came crashing through the bedroom window, feet first. All six of them.

I instantly turned myself into a praying mantis's worst nightmare: a very hungry, extremely large monkey. Not all the way to King Kong. Just thirteen feet tall. In other words, I was *double* the size of The Prayer.

I could've gone with a giant bird, snake, bat, or frog. They all prey on mantis meat. I chose the monkey because I like the way they laugh.

Feeling threatened for the first time since forever, Number 1 stood tall and spread its forelegs wide. Wings fanned out from its bubble butt. Its mouth flew open in a silent scream.

The creep looked like a catcher ready to catch a baseball without a glove.

Which gave me an idea.

I smashed a giant monkey fist up into that ceiling hole and ripped out a nasty chunk of nail-spiked two-by-four. I cocked back that stick of lumber like a baseball bat. When I swung for the fences, Number 1 shot out a pincer paw and, Mr. Miyagi-style, grabbed it one-handed in midair.

Then he crushed my weapon into a powdery cloud of sawdust.

Level 11 strength? It's off the charts because it's *off the charts.*

The Prayer started working its moist mouth back and forth, revealing all sorts of razor-sharp cutting components that a normal, garden-variety praying mantis would use to grind through all the tough insect shells in its daily diet. Number 1, on the other hand, would use its razor-sharp grinders on me.

"Buh-bye, Monkey Boy," it gloated.

I lunged forward, ready to bite its head off.

But my prey disappeared.

Suddenly, the *Star Wars* wallpaper lining my childhood bedroom started to move. The curtains and window frame, too.

That's when I realized that Number 1 was using a praying mantis's incredible camouflage skills to blend into the background the way a chameleon would.

I morphed out of my monkey suit and backed up a step or two.

The walls of the bedroom kept wavering. The Prayer was coming at me. Setting up its final deadly strike.

I kept backing up, even though I was pretty certain this wasn't the kind of backup plan my dad had in mind.

Suddenly, things weren't looking so good for me—or this planet.

And I had a sinking feeling that I'd be the one sent first into the black hole of oblivion.

Chapter 52

IT WAS TIME to change tactics.

Plan A had been to outmuscle and outfight Number 1. So far, that wasn't working out so well.

Once again, my father's words came echoing back to me, and I was glad I listened.

Time for Plan B.

Instead of bringing the pain to The Prayer, I'd let The Prayer be the one to lay down the hurt. It was time to try something crazy.

Using my internal Wi-Fi, I quickly downloaded everything the Internet had on mantids, which—I learned—was the proper plural for mantis.

Interesting fact. But it wouldn't do me much good in a final fight to the death.

I also learned that the female mantis will often eat the male after mating because the extra protein boost from her husband's carcass helps her eggs develop.

Unfortunately, there was no Mrs. Prayer to jump in and chomp off Number 1's head.

However, the Internet search confirmed what I had already learned from experience: mantids are voracious eaters, always on the lookout for food. They live life with a very simple plan: Hunt. Eat. Hunt. Eat.

I needed to take advantage of that primal instinct.

So, just as Number 1 shed its cloak of camouflage and swung its forelegs at my head, I pulled another quick change.

This time, I turned myself into a tasty treat that The Prayer couldn't resist but wouldn't have a chance of catching: a big, juicy housefly the size of a bloated softball.

Stringy drool dribbled down from the thing's garbage-disposal mouth.

It was hungry for fly.

When it made a grab for me, I flitted away before its vise grip could crush me.

When it lunged again, I buzzed around inside its flapping dreadlocks.

Number 1 went berserk trying to shoo me out of its hairy head. All six limbs were flailing. His skull did a 359-degree spin on its spindly neck. When it spun back the other way, its limbs got all tangled up together, and the giant beast fell on its bulbous butt, spraining its wings.

I hovered over his head for an instant—making like the circling stars when a cartoon gets walloped. Then, skimming across its antennae to make sure it could smell how good dinner would taste if it ever caught me, I zipped out the bedroom door.

The Prayer chased after me, its giant limbs clomping down the steps. It reminded me of that brainless dinosaur skeleton that had chased me and my friends around the American Museum of Natural History all those nights ago.

The Prayer was doing what its instincts told it to do.

It was hunting me. Relentlessly.

It was tearing through walls, smashing out windows, punching holes in drywall, chasing me around and around the backyard.

Number 1 was an excellent tracker. But it wasn't doing a very good job of getting to the "eat" part of "hunt, eat, hunt, eat."

Because to eat me, it had to catch me.

And that just wasn't going to happen. Not that day. Not in Kansas. Because I was a fly with swifter moves than a hummingbird stoked on ten gallons of pure maple syrup.

Chapter 53

ONCE AGAIN, I wondered if Mikaela was watching from her heavenly perch, because for this battle I had definitely chosen flight over fight.

I wasn't running away from the danger. I was just trying to wear the danger down so it wouldn't be quite so dangerous. I was hoping to nudge Number 1's Level 11 strength down into the single digits.

And it looked like my plan was working.

The Prayer's gnarly red dreadlocks were dribbling droplets like waterlogged anchor ropes. The beast was breathing hard. Its asparagus stalk of a body kept bellowing in and out.

Meanwhile, I kept flitting, floating, and fleeing all night and into the early hours of the morning. The Prayer never stopped chasing me. We went trampling through the old farmhouse so many times, there wasn't much left of it besides a pile of smoldering rubble and a freestanding fireplace and chimney. Number 1 had bashed down all the walls in his quest for what it wanted: *me*.

I took a few pit stops, now and then, to replenish my energy by grabbing a bite to eat. The rotting fast-food garbage littering the sides of the road became my Quick Pick Mini Mart.

Yes, it was gross. Especially when you realize a fly can only eat liquids. They turn solid foods into a liquid by spitting or vomiting on it. After that, they use their tongue like a straw to suck the slop up.

After a while, I decided I'd just go hungry and skip the moldy french fries and rancid Whoppers with half-chewed lettuce and tomatoes until after I defeated The Prayer.

Yes, I wanted to eat. And, believe it or not, garbage smells great when you're a fly. But always getting what you want—when you want it—is a horrible way to live your life. Especially if what you want is no good for you, or if it constantly escapes your grasp.

For The Prayer, I was a little of both.

He couldn't quite catch me.

And even if he did, I definitely wouldn't agree with his stomach. The second he swallowed my fly body, I'd pull one of my classic moves and morph back into being a full-sized teenage boy, which would definitely bust open his gullet.

You see, my father taught me to fight with my head as much as my hands.

No way could I ever beat The Prayer in any kind of

hand-to-hand combat or martial arts duel. Not even if I summoned up Joe, Willy, Dana, and Emma. The Prayer would outmuscle all of us combined.

To beat this brute, I had to count on the muscle in my head.

Chapter 54

FINALLY, ABOUT THREE hours after dawn, The Prayer's knobby knees buckled.

The lanky creature crumbled to the ground.

"Enough!" it cried.

I hovered six feet in front of his face. I know mantids have incredible eyesight. So it could probably see the huge garbage-eating grin on my fuzzy face.

But then it did something I should have expected.

It materialized an Opus 24/24.

The weapon whined, signaling that it was fully charged. The Prayer aimed the thing at me.

He was going to swat a fly with a bazooka blast.

I could dodge the shot, but the shockwave would send out thermal waves of incredible turbulence, making the air impossible for me to navigate through.

So I decided to fight fire with fire.

I could've materialized my own Opus 24/24 and blasted

him before he blasted me. But I had something better in mind.

"Wait!" I squeaked in a tiny fly voice as I made the switch back to my own body.

"You've obviously won," I said. "Let me make this easy for you."

I raised both my arms and opened them wide, giving The Prayer an easy shot at my heart.

"This is the first smart move you have made, Danny Boy. I will make your death swift and clean, yet excruciatingly painful."

I just grinned. "Go for it."

I saw him twist a knob. The weapon's molecular resonator wailed a shrill, high-pitched squeal that kept screeching higher and higher.

I zoomed my eyes in on Number 1's trigger pincer.

"Say hello to your mommy and daddy for me on the other side, Danny Boy!"

The serrated limb budged back half a millimeter.

I instantly threw time into superslow mo so I'd have half a second to materialize my weapon: a four-by-four sheet of extremely reflective and totally impenetrable adamantite, a rare green metal found only in the mines on the planet Ramdon Nine.

The adamantite shield would block my body. It also fit perfectly in my outstretched hands.

I let go of my grip on time. The Opus 24/24 exploded with a deafening roar.

A plasma pulse of pure, blue-white pain erupted from

its muzzle. I felt it hammer into my adamantite shield, making it shimmy. But then the pulse ricocheted off the adamantite and rebounded onto The Prayer.

Number 1 squealed in shock and agony. He had just shot himself in the foot. All six of them.

He collapsed on his brittle back. I heard a snapping crackle and then the muffled sound of squishy splats. I figured the giant's internal organs were turning into mush. For a moment, its spindly legs kicked helplessly at the air as it writhed in horrendous pain.

Because Number 1 had just taken on itself all the pain and hurt it had meant to send my way.

It's why the reflecting shield was a better idea than any weapon I could have possibly conjured up.

I knew that The Prayer, cruelest monster to ever set crooked foot on planet Earth, would crank up the pain resonator in that godforsaken weapon all the way to *its* Level 11: Eternal Damnation.

That's why the monster was now dying the worst death its own twisted mind could ever have imagined.

Chapter 55

NUMBER 1 WAS dead.

I don't know what I expected.

Fireworks. Marching bands. Maybe a ticker tape parade down New York's canyon of heroes.

I had just completed my life's mission. I had avenged my parents' deaths. I had done what I had come to this planet to do.

I swiped my fingers across one of the pentagram panels on my dad's old Tusk computer and initiated a video call to Special Agent Judge at FBI headquarters in D.C.

"Number 1 has been zeroed out, sir," I reported.

"It's gone?" asked Agent Judge, overjoyed. "You're positive?"

I rotated the Tusk sideways so he could see the petrified and still smoldering husk of what had once been the most ferocious alien outlaw to ever land on Terra Firma.

"Behold his earthly remains," I said sarcastically. "He doesn't look so fierce lying on his back with his legs splayed out, does he? Kind of reminds me of an 'after' pic in a bug spray commercial."

"Thank you, Daniel," said Mr. Judge, emotion choking his voice.

And it was emotion he was definitely entitled to. The Prayer had killed his wife right after the putrid thing murdered my parents.

"You have no idea how long I have waited for this day, Daniel."

I could've answered, "Yes, sir. I do." Instead I just nodded and let him have a moment to savor the sweet sensation of justice finally been served.

There was one more thing I had to tell him.

"Sir," I said, "rest assured, I will find Mel, no matter where Number 1 hid her."

Mr. Judge looked confused. "What do you mean, Daniel?"

"Now that Number 1 is no longer a threat to humanity, my sole focus will be locating and extracting your daughter from her current hostage situation. The Prayer may have a few henchbeasts guarding her, but…"

"Daniel?"

"Sir?"

"I'm not sure what you're talking about. Like I said when you came to visit me in D.C., Mel's safe. She's at the horse ranch. In Kentucky. Hang on. I'll patch her in." Agent Judge clacked his keyboard.

A second pentagram panel flickered to life on my Tusk computer.

"Hey, Daniel."

It was Mel—looking more beautifully radiant than ever (and not just because she wasn't clamping electrodes to my ankles anymore, either). Relief flooded through me. Apparently, the whole kidnapping and torture thing had been a sick and twisted mental movie planted in my head by the late Number 1. He had even made me question Mel's loyalty and goodness. No doubt about it, IT was good.

Was being the key word.

"Are you okay?" Mel asked from her tiny screen.

"Never better," I said with a smile.

Because it was true. My work on Terra Firma was finally done.

Except...

"Sir?" I said to Agent Judge's image. "Any word on that black hole?"

"No news."

"Is it still growing?"

"Hang on." He clacked more computer keys. "Interesting."

"What?"

"When did you terminate Number 1?"

"Five, maybe ten, minutes ago."

Mr. Judge grinned. "That's what I figured. According to our friends at NASA, that's exactly when the anomaly slowed its rate of expansion."

"Way to go, Daniel!" said Mel, my personal cheerleader. "You just saved Earth's bacon."

"Thanks," I said through half a laugh. "But, sir?"

"Yes, Daniel?"

"Is it still growing?"

"Slightly. Guess Number 1 put his anomaly on autopilot."

"Something you and your marvelous imagination should be able to take care of," said Mel. "Right, Daniel?"

"No doubt. But, since there's no imminent threat or danger, I have a more important operation to plan."

"What's that?" asked Mr. Judge, sounding slightly concerned.

"Organizing a little party, sir. We need to celebrate. It's not every day you get to wipe out your worst enemy and save the planet at the same time. Mel?"

"Yes, Daniel?"

"I'll pick you up at seven."

"You have a car?"

I shrugged. "I could, I guess. Any make or model you like."

"Um, Daniel—you don't have a driver's license."

"True. Besides, it'll be more fun if we teleport together."

Chapter 56

AS PROMISED, I picked Mel up at 7 PM.

Literally.

I teleported to Kentucky, wrapped both my arms around her waist, hoisted her off the ground, and two blinks later we were back in Kansas.

I had, of course, totally rebuilt the farmhouse, putting it back into mint condition. I had even planted a couple of rose bushes in the front yard and a whole field of Kansas wildflowers in the back.

Number 1's carcass? Long gone.

After a quick laser-based cremation, I whipped together a mini-funnel cloud and scattered his ashes up beyond the stratosphere, in that layer where the molecules and atoms have a hard time reconnecting.

"Where's the grub?" said Joe, who—of course—I had summoned to Kansas for the party.

"Inside," said Emma. "And Joe? There are organic carrot sticks, celery stalks, and cherry tomatoes."

Joe cocked an eyebrow. "And your point is?"

"You don't have to stuff yourself on corn dog cupcakes, moo-oink balls, deep-fried cookie dough, or red velvet funnel cakes, which—if you don't mind me saying, Daniel—look a lot like congealed intestines."

(For my little party, I had recreated several of the crazier foods from last year's Kansas State Fair, including moo-oink balls, which are juicy meatballs wrapped in greasy bacon.)

"That's why I made the veggie platter," I said.

"Waste of time, bro," said Joe, heading into the house. "Waste. Of. Time."

Emma's big brother, Willy, came over, nibbling a row of potato chips on a wooden skewer, another food-tent treat from the state fair.

"I like this," he said. "When you're done snacking, you have a weapon."

"Right," said Mel, with a laugh. "You could poke out somebody's eye with that thing."

"I could." Willy munched another chip. "But I'd wait till all the potato chips were gone."

Dana was at the party, too, of course, only she wasn't physically there because Mel already was.

I know. The whole soul mate thing confuses me, too. Xanthos, who was in the backyard nibbling on some of the tastier wildflowers, promised he'd walk me through the conceptual overview later.

"Later works for me," I had said. "Because tonight is all about having fun."

I felt like the munchkins must've felt in that movie about The Wizard of Oz. *Ding-dong, The Prayer was dead!* It was time to party.

We had music blasting (I had cooked up a couple of awesome DJs for the night). There was a ton of food and drink in the house. Most importantly, all my amazing friends and comrades in arms were there. We laughed and joked and shared war stories about all the aliens we had hunted down together. And then we danced.

Well, everybody except Joe.

Nothing could tear him away from the state fair–style food after he had sampled his first Krispy Kreme burger à la mode: a hamburger sandwiched between two glazed Krispy Kremes with a scoop of vanilla ice cream plopped in the top doughnut hole.

You have done well, little brudda, said Xanthos (in my head, of course) when things started winding down around midnight. *Remember—never give sway to the negative way, mon.*

Thanks, I said.

I escorted Mel home to Kentucky (her dad had given her a pretty lenient curfew of 1 AM because he knew we had a lot to celebrate) and then I returned to Kansas.

"I want to spend one last night in that house," I told Mel. "One night knowing all the horrible things that happened there can never happen again."

"Go for it," she said. Then she gave me a quick kiss on the lips. It tasted sweeter than the deep-fried Kool-Aid they serve at the Kansas State Fair.

I closed my eyes when we kissed a second time.

When I opened them, I was back in Kansas. In my bed-room. And, for the first time since I was three years old, I felt totally safe.

I drifted off to sleep; the best sleep I'd had in over a decade.

Or, at least it was—until I started to dream.

Chapter 57

IN MY DREAM, I was standing in the backyard of my Kansas home with Mikaela. Only this time, she wasn't costumed as a college girl or a karate expert.

She was dressed in a flowing white robe that shimmered and sparkled like an angel on top of a Christmas tree. Four gossamer wings glowed warmly as they fluttered on her back.

"It is not done," she whispered in my ear. "It is never over."

She reached out her hand. I took it. Together, we shot up into the sky like streaking comets. In the dream, my own body began to glow and I joined Mikaela as one of several stars twinkling in a sprawling constellation.

"Look," I heard her voice cry out. "See!"

Dozens of light years away from Earth and its solar system, I had a pretty good view of what was going on in the Milky Way.

I could see the black hole sucking nearby planets, meteoroid, and stars into a swirling wormhole of nothingness.

The hole was tinged deep purple around its rim.

"It is gathering new strength," whispered Mikaela's voice. "It is not finished with you."

"Number 1?" I asked.

"Number 1 is insignificant."

"How can you say that?" I demanded. "Number 1 killed my parents. Number 1 killed Mel's mom. Number 1 incited all the other alien outlaws to bring their evil to Earth. Number 1 tortured me and hunted me and tortured me again. How can that, in any way, be called insignificant?"

"That wasn't Number 1."

"Um, yes it was." Yeah, I was getting a little snarky with the glittery angel because she was making me mad. "Trust me. I know what I'm talking about because I'm the guy the big bug was torturing."

"Number 1, the alien creature you knew as The Prayer, was but a vessel, Daniel. The most recent host for the spirit of eternal evil."

Now my dream flashed back to my father's Tusk computer. I was holding it in my palm near the salt marsh. My dream was giving me an instant replay—so that I'd pay closer attention to what my dad's backup computer had been trying to tell me the first time, I guess:

"The creature known as The Prayer, currently operating on Terra Firma in the guise of an overgrown praying mantis, is the most evil alien outlaw of the current millennium."

In the guise of an overgrown praying mantis.

In other words, The Prayer was a costume that the force we call Evil or whatever had decided to wear for a while.

Xanthos had said basically the same thing. He had called The Prayer a "highly refined manifestation of eternal, omnipresent, and omnipotent evil."

My dream was making something extremely clear: I had not eliminated the threat of evil when I destroyed The Prayer. I had simply shattered its most recent body.

IT, the *real* Number 1, was still out there.

Mikaela's voice washed over me again: "It is not through with you, Daniel. It may *never* be through with you."

In a flash, the dream shifted scenes again.

I was back inside the farmhouse in Kansas.

But I wasn't in my bedroom. I was down in the basement molding the Seven Wonders of the Ancient World with Play-Doh.

I was three years old again.

And I knew the cellar door was just about to be kicked open.

Chapter 58

EVEN THOUGH I knew it was a dream, the terror felt extremely real.

I guess nightmares always do.

"Focus here," whispered Mikaela's gentle voice in my head.

Watch with your soul, my yute, added Xanthos in his lilting island tones. *See what is truly before your eyes.*

I'll try, I thought back.

I let the memory unspool. Let it play out precisely as I had chronicled it in my memory banks:

I'm trembling and pressing my small, vulnerable body up against an old water heater, petrified about what just happened to my mom and dad. A beam of violet-tinged light shines down the stairs into the basement.

Freeze frame!

Was that the answer?

That before I saw The Prayer, I saw a beam of violet-tinged light?

That's what had been extra vivid in my most recent recollections of that horrible day all those years ago. The violet-tinged light.

I thought about Xanthos and Mikaela, how the two of them were always bathed in the orange-red warmth of the sun, even on cloudy days.

"This is the color of the Legions of the Light," my father's computer had informed me. "The color of confidence and creative power. This is your color."

On the other hand, the purple light that had preceded Number 1 into my childhood basement was the polar opposite; it lurked down at the dark, ultraviolet end of the spectrum.

Then I thought about the swath of violet-tinged light that crept across the hospital floor a half instant before The Prayer burst in to blast my parents and Pork Chop. Okay. The bad guys' team color was purple.

Still dreaming, my memory scrubbed forward a few frames:

And then I saw it—a six-and-a-half-foot-tall praying mantis. That terrible form...

That last thought echoed in my ears.

Even as a three-year-old, I had suspected what I now knew to be true: Zeboul, the force of ultimate evil that exists in the universe, had taken on the "terrible *form*" of The Prayer that night in Kansas—and all through my dangerous days as the alien hunter—because it knew the shape would terrify me.

But that didn't mean it couldn't take on other forms even more menacing.

Mikaela was right: It wasn't done doing evil on this planet.

It wasn't done with me, either.

Chapter 59

WHEN I WOKE up, my bed sheets were soaked with sweat.

The real Number 1 was still out there; it would *always* be out there. It was a force of nature as old as the universe itself, fueling all sorts of wickedness and worse. Also, it still wanted to destroy the planet.

Why?

I had a theory: It was ticked off because too many earthlings fought against evil by doing good. Every time you collect cans of food for hungry people at your school, Evil has a bad day. When you stand up to a bully picking on a kid half his size, Evil sits in a corner and sulks. Even when you toss a bottle into a recycling bin instead of an ordinary trash can, Evil gets steamed.

It just can't stand the fact that good people on this planet are always standing up for what's right. Not everybody, of course. But enough to tip Terra Firma's scales toward being a "good world" instead of an "evil playground."

I had a hunch that the eternal and all-powerful evil some called Zeboul seriously wanted to tip the galactic balance in its favor: it wanted to suck Terra Firma's entire solar system into an endless black hole. That meant I had to do everything in my considerable power to patch up that galaxy-busting sinkhole before it grew wide enough to wolf down my adopted home.

But how on Earth (or any other planet) was I going to take on an elemental force of the universe? How could one teenager possibly wipe out evil?

My dad was right. I was definitely going to need major backup.

It was time to summon the gang and put together a plan.

I remembered something else the Tusk computer had said in its mini-lecture: "Wherever you find negative energy you will also find its positive opposite." Somehow, we'd have to tap into the plus side of the eternal energy equation. And fast.

I focused on my friends.

But they didn't come. Instead, I felt a strange sensation, like some sort of invisible but extremely powerful force closing in around me.

And whatever the strange force was, I could tell that it definitely wasn't playing for the good guys.

And that's when the torture started.

Chapter 60

I FELT SUCH intense pressure in my head that I thought my skull might implode. A powerful, throbbing fist was squeezing my whole body, crushing the air out of my lungs.

I tried one more time to call for backup, to summon my friends. But my brain pulsed with excruciating waves of big-time hurt whenever I tried to ignite my imagination.

As you know, I have felt extraordinary pain during my years as an Alien Hunter.

I have been beaten, battered, and bruised.

I have faced unrelenting torture and the brutalizing burn of alien weaponry blasts.

But, trust me on this—I have never, *ever* felt pain this intense.

My overwhelming agony cut through my body and went straight for my soul. I wondered if I had wasted my entire life chasing after a shadow monster. I had not avenged my parents' deaths by destroying The Prayer because the big bug was only a small pawn in an eternal struggle that had gone on since the dawn of time.

The pain was paralyzing. Once again, I wanted to die, if only to escape this profound and unimaginably intense torment.

I squeezed my eyes shut in utter despair.

At first I saw exploding white circles haloed with flares of white light—like flash bulbs of pain popping against the back of my eyelids with every beat of my heart.

And then everything went black.

No.

Black-tinged violet.

That's when I knew the true Number 1—the eternal, disembodied essence of undiluted Evil—had my heart and soul locked firmly in its grip.

Chapter 61

I COULD FEEL the sinister thing probing my mind. It was shutting down good memories, stirring up horrible fears. Toying with my emotions and shoving me toward self-pity.

Then the wretched beast started gibbering at me in piercing blips, communicating with the screech of binary computer code. Fortunately—or maybe unfortunately—whatever brain cells controlled my internal universal translator were still fully functional. I got to hear every ugly thought the unseen fiend shot my way.

"I want to show you something that might be beyond your infantile comprehension," it said. In translation, the voice sounded as dark and malicious as the spirit behind it. Think Darth Vader, Voldemort, or a window-rattling bass line. "Watch carefully, Daniel. Behold your fate."

My mind's eye was overwhelmed with a digitally enhanced 3-D IMAX version of that horrible night in Kansas. Once again, I was a small boy hiding behind a water heater in the basement. Once again, The Prayer came stalking down the steps with its Opus 24/24, hunting me.

"But you never saw what was going on upstairs, did you, Daniel?" rumbled the malevolent voice invading my mind.

Suddenly, the scene shifted. Like a floating camera flying downfield to cover the action in a football game, my mind's eye flew up the staircase and straight through the cellar door.

I saw something I had never seen before and never want to see again: Both my parents writhing on the ground in unbearable agony and pain.

"Neither one died right away," gloated the voice. "Oh, no. Where's the pleasure in that? While you were turning into a tick and fleeing the scene, they were upstairs suffering for a long, long, *long* time. If I remember correctly, and I always do, your mother actually prayed for death because the end of her miserable little life would have been such a blessing."

I wished I could close my eyes, cut off this horrendous vision of both my parents twitching on the floor, their mouths open wide as they cried out silent screams. But I couldn't. The scene was firmly planted in my head by the demon that had taken over my mind and memories. There was no way to pull the plug and shut this horror movie down.

"I was inside their minds, Daniel, just like I'm inside yours right now. This pain you feel? They felt worse. Soon you will, too. You will beg for mercy, and just like your mother you will pray for death."

And somehow, impossibly, the pain intensified.

The dark presence felt like a giant tumor devouring my brain, pushing it sideways, squashing it up against the hard lining of my skull. It was growing exponentially.

There was no way to stop it. No way to keep my head from exploding.

I knew the dark and awful truth: In a few more seconds, I would be dead.

My soul would be crushed.

Daniel X would cease to exist.

Chapter 62

BUT EVIL WASN'T done with me.

It wanted me to die regretting every choice I had ever made in my life.

"You were foolish enough to think these humans were worthy of your protection, Alien Hunter? You wasted your life trying to save this planet when those who inhabit it have done everything in their power to destroy it?"

Now my pain-racked mind swirled with images of smokestacks chugging out swollen clouds of black soot. Oil spills suffocating pelicans and fish. Birds circling heaped mountains of rotting garbage. Fluorescent green chemicals oozing out of a drain pipe into a rippling stream. Rivers burning.

There...is...good.... I struggled to complete the thought despite the pain. *I...have...seen...the good.*

"You saw what you wanted to see, foolish boy. See the truth: humanity reigns as the most colossal mistake in all of creation. It is a race of greedy, avaricious, selfish animals determined to destroy all the lesser creatures doomed to share this puny planet with them."

I knew it was trying to play mind games with me. It would be delighted to watch me die, totally lamenting my decision to join the Alpar Nokian Protectorship. I had forsaken any chance at a halfway normal teenage life to defend Terra Firma and its human inhabitants from an onslaught of alien outlaws.

What if they hadn't been worth it?

What if my whole life had been a colossal waste of time?

The only thing worse than dying, I guess, is living a life with absolutely no meaning.

But I refused to wallow in the hideous thing's dark and gloomy shadows. I clung to the truth as I knew it: There *was* good in this world. I had seen it. I had tasted it. I had heard it. Despite all their flaws, earthlings (and their planet) were definitely worth saving.

So, with every minuscule ounce of my remaining strength, I fought back. I punched through the pain and countered the evil thing's thoughts with a few of my own:

If these humans are so evil, why don't you embrace them instead of sending them off to oblivion in your black hole?

It hesitated.

The irrefutable logic of my argument caused a momentary glitch in its operating system.

Its grip of pain loosened.

Not much.

But enough.

I was out of there in a flash.

Chapter 63

MY WORLD WAS all in my head, now. And the forces of darkness were crowded in there with me, big-time.

I could feel the violet-tinged, tumorous thing regaining strength after its momentary power drop.

So I tried dipping back in time to see if I could shake it out of my head with a quantum leap.

I zipped back to Monday, March 4, 1861. Washington, D.C. Abraham Lincoln's first inaugural address on the steps of the Capitol, which was still under construction. I would force Zeboul to listen to true humanity:

"We are not enemies, but friends," Lincoln declared. "We must not be enemies. Though passion may have strained it must not break our bonds of affection. The mystic chords of memory...will yet swell when again touched, as surely they will be, by the better angels of our nature."

"He'll be dead a month after his second inaugural," rumbled up the voice of Evil. "John Wilkes Booth was a good and loyal servant of mine. So was Lee Harvey Oswald. So were all the killers and torturers throughout the ages."

I went back through the ages and hit the highlights of human history. The signing of the Magna Carta. Gutenberg inventing the printing press. Mozart's father buying his son a piano.

But for every good vision I conjured up, the evil force countered with something equally horrendous. The Spanish Inquisition. Adolph Hitler. The mushroom cloud of an atomic blast.

With each of these small historical downfalls where bad had bested good, the gnarled knot of darkness grew larger, blotting out more and more of life's light.

And while it expanded, doubling then tripling its size, it laughed.

"You are such a child, Daniel. An infant clinging to the illusion of goodness and light. What a pity you'll never grow older and wiser and see this wretched world for what it really is: a place of greed and sloth and cowardice."

I flew into the future, hoping to glimpse some wondrous day when the world lived in peace and harmony.

But the darkness was overtaking me.

I couldn't see that bright and shining day.

There was only encroaching night and the evil one laughing at me.

Laughing and laughing and laughing.

Chapter 64

AND THEN THERE was only blackness and a tiny dot of light, as if someone had pricked a pin through a thick sheet of black paper.

When I focused on that glowing point, it started to widen. Slowly at first, then with gathering speed.

My pain decreased.

Now it was as if I were walking down a fun house tube of swirling blackness. I was drawn like a mindless moth toward the warm, golden light that lured me to the shaft's far end.

As I drew closer to the light streaming at me like a train beacon in a mountain tunnel, I felt amazingly peaceful.

Every drop of pain was gone.

I remembered some of my dad's funnier jokes.

I smelled pancakes. My mom's pancakes. The best in the galaxy.

Silhouettes of familiar figures slowly emerged in the

dusty beam and beckoned for me to move closer. As I did, I could vaguely make out the faces.

My father and mother. My grandparents. Joe, Willy, and Emma. Even Pork Chop.

"Where's Dana?" I asked.

"Why do you seek the living among the dead?" asked earth-mother Emma.

Right. Dana's soul had passed through death and returned to life in the person of Melody Judge.

Death.

That made me freeze.

In fact, I retreated half a step.

"Am I about to die?" I asked.

Behind me, I could hear the evil one's laughter.

My mother extended her hand. "It's over, Daniel. You fought the good fight. Step across the line. Join us on the other side."

I looked down and saw a thin golden line faintly visible through the wispy fog shrouding the tunnel's floor.

Behind me, the demon's laughter boomed.

"No, Mom. I have to go back. They need me."

My father stepped forward. "And you need to join us, son. Now."

"Come on, Daniel," cried my wingman, Willy. "It's okay. Honest. We've already scoped it out for you."

"And the food's fantastic," added Joe.

"But, Dad," I said, "I still need to find my backup."

He grinned. "You don't need backup anymore, son."

"Come along, Daniel," said my mother as she and the

others turned and started walking into the tunnel, leading the way into the welcoming warmth of the light. I heard music. *The Symphony of the Departed*. It was being played by an Alpar Nokian orchestra. "Everybody's waiting for you."

"It's bigger than Gathering Day!" added Joe, as he began to disappear into the light.

"But..." I stammered.

"Death comes to all of us, Daniel," said my father as he, too, whited out and faded away. "Now you must come to it."

I took one tentative step forward. When I did, the evil thing suddenly stopped laughing. In fact, it started screaming.

Something had definitely changed.

So I took another step.

It shrieked even louder.

That settled it. If my death could make that horrible monster miserable, I was ready to die.

I stepped across the glimmering line and into the light.

Chapter 65

I WAS LETTING myself die.

Letting go of life. Looking forward to whatever waited for me up ahead in the light-filled tunnel.

My whole life flashed before my eyes. My time as a baby on Alpar Nok. Riding the roller coaster at the Kansas State Fair. My first ice cream cone.

I saw all the cute girls I've ever had a crush on. That was nice.

I saw Mel and me meeting for the first time. In Kentucky. I'd been riding on Xanthos but ended up on my butt in a very cold creek.

"Ride much?" she'd said with a laugh.

And I was instantly head-over-heels, wackaloon crazy about her.

I flashed back to my time in Portland. Los Angeles. London. Stonehenge. Tokyo.

I remembered my days time-traveling into Terra

Firma's past. Hanging out with Merlin, the medieval magician. Chatting with Benjamin Franklin and George Washington.

Then I saw all sorts of wonderful memories of my home planet, Alpar Nok. The gunjun flowers blossoming in the high mountain plains. The Bryn Spi Symphony Orchestra. Me riding on the back of Chordata, this gigantic telepathic elephant. Spending time with my grandmother, Blaleen. Uncle Kraffleprog calling me "stinky boy."

Next I saw some of my earliest memories. Joe, Willy, Dana, Emma, and me in preschool playing in a sandbox. That was the start of our "drang"—an intense friendship bond that kept us eternally linked, even when one or all of us died. Those scenes were probably my favorite ones in my whole life. My "drang" and I sure shared a lot of laughs—like that night we took over a whole amusement park and rode all the rides, even to places they were never meant to go.

Happily, the part of my life where I hunted aliens or they hunted me was condensed to a ten-second "greatest hits" clip collage of mayhem, explosions, martial arts lessons from my dad, and monsters dying. I was glad when that section of my life review was over because I was done with all that.

I was dead.

Up ahead I saw a white light that was more brilliantly intense than any I had ever seen.

I flew straight into the welcoming comfort of the light's glorious embrace.

Soon, there was nothing but the light. Peaceful. Tranquil. It engulfed me.

I let my memories drift away.

Chapter 66

AS I PASSED through the light, I felt my mind overflowing with all the knowledge in the universe.

Everything I had ever wanted to know, I now knew. It was as if every library and database in galaxies far and near had instantly downloaded their entire treasure trove of information directly into my brain.

"Welcome, Daniel." A new voice was inside my head. Mikaela. Soft and comforting. "You are truly one with the light, now."

"And it feels amazing!" I said, giggling like a giddy kid who's just tasted his very first cherry snow cone.

"Because you're not alone anymore, Daniel. You have joined the spirits of the departed. You will never be lonely again."

She was right. For most of my life, I had basically been an orphan. My friends and family were all dead. They only came to me through the power of my imagination. Now I had come to *them*. We were all dead.

Except, of course, the girl of my dreams: Dana who had become Mel.

I poked around in my brain's new supersized knowledge center but I couldn't find the one answer I was searching for.

"How was Dana's soul able to return to life?" I asked.

"Those who live in the light never truly die, Daniel."

"Wait a second. Are you saying *I* could go back?"

"If you have an overwhelmingly compelling reason to do so, yes. You can elect to return to life instead of moving on, as your father and mother chose to do."

"Where are they now?"

"Once you cast their souls to the wind, Daniel, they became free of this circle and journeyed on to the next realm where they eagerly wait for you to join them."

"They can't return to the life they once knew?"

"Not without jeopardizing their eternal souls. They have moved on to the next dimension, Daniel. For them, turning back would be extremely risky."

"But Dana went back to be with me," I said.

"Such was her choice," answered Mikaela. "She knew she was your soul mate. That you two were destined to be together, across all time and dimension."

"Then I have to go back, too."

"Do you have a compelling reason, Daniel?"

"I have two: Mel and Terra Firma."

"If you wait a while longer, both will soon join you here."

"You mean when Earth gets sucked into that black hole

230

and every creature on the planet, including my soul mate, dies?"

"Precisely."

"Yeah, that's not gonna fly. I know I could move on, that my parents are waiting for me, but I need to go back. Sorry."

"Ah. So, once again, you choose fight over flight?"

"Guess some things never change. Even after we die."

"Well, if you're going back," said Willy, whose spirit was suddenly at my side, "we're coming with you."

Okay, this is weird. In all that bright, white light, I couldn't actually *see* Willy. I could only feel him. And I don't mean "feel" like I was holding out my hands playing blind man's bluff and feeling his face because I didn't really have hands anymore. I could just *feel* his presence. I could totally grok him.

"Dana is our friend, too," added Emma, her ethereal spirit joining us in the light. "We want to go back into life with you, Daniel."

"Besides," said Joe, who was there, too, "it'd be cool to actually *be* alive again instead of just popping in and out of your imagination all the time. For one thing, we could eat on a much more regular basis."

"We all want to go back, Mikaela," I said. "We *need* to go back. Dana and a very nice planet, neither of which really deserve to die, are depending on us."

"Very well," said the angelic voice. "But before you depart, know that all who have passed through death into the light return to life with enhanced abilities."

"Really?" said Joe. "Like superpowers? Cool."

"Will we be able to do all the stuff that Daniel does?" asked Emma.

"Perhaps," answered Mikaela mysteriously. "It will be for each of you to discover what your new talents and potential might be."

And then it hit me: this is why Number 1 or Zeboul or whatever name Evil was giving itself these days didn't want to kill me.

This is why it kept sending me off to that crazy, make-believe hospital or torturing me instead of slaying me.

This is why it screeched in terror and fled the instant I decided to step over that quivering line and die.

It knew I might choose to come back from the other side.

That, if I died, I might come back bigger and badder than ever.

What it didn't know was this: I'd be bringing my three butt-kicking friends with me, too!

Chapter 67

I GASPED AND breathed as deeply as I could.

I sucked in oxygen like you do when you pop out of the deep end of a swimming pool after you've been sitting on the bottom, trying to set a new personal record for how long you can hold your breath.

My eyes were still blinded by the light.

But I realized it was only because I was facing due east, staring straight into Earth's blazing sun.

I was back among the living. I was standing on the surface of the earth breathing fresh, delicious, absolutely amazing air.

I looked to my left and right.

I was holding hands with Joe and Willy. Willy was hanging on to Emma's hand, too.

I had brought my friends back to life with me.

And my friends were all totally real. I could tell. Don't ask me exactly how, I just could. My three friends, standing by my side in the newly mown lawn of my rebuilt

Kansas home, were more real than any hyper-real copy of them I had ever called forth using mentally rearranged molecules.

"Mmm," said Emma, taking in her own deep breath of fresh air. "It smells amazing. Flowers, grass, honeysuckle. Terra Firma has incredible scents."

"This is absolutely awesome, you guys!" said Willy, shaking loose from our handhold so he could slap me a finger-tingling high-five. "*Feels* awesome, too!" He flexed and stretched out his digits, marveling at how incredible it was to be alive again, to be inside a fully functional body.

While I laughed at Willy's admiration for his own fingers, I heard Joe chomping on something behind me. I also smelled a meatball hero smothered in marinara sauce and mozzarella cheese.

"So, Daniel," said Joe, his mouth full of mashed meat and bread, "you know that amazingly fantastic thing you do where you whip up a whole meal out of thin air?"

"Yeah?" I said with a smile because I knew where he was going.

"I'm right behind you, bro. I can already do main courses. Just need to concentrate on side dishes."

Now I smelled deep-fried onion rings.

"There we go!" said Joe.

"How about teleporting?"

I couldn't believe my eyes. Mel came bopping out the front door of the farmhouse to stand on the porch.

"Can any of you guys do that one?"

"You can?" I stammered.

Mel shrugged. "Well, after we did it together last night, I went ahead and tried it myself."

"You picked it up after watching me do it once?"

Okay. I was slightly annoyed. Teleporting took me like *forever* to learn.

"I had a good teacher," said Mel, with a wink and a smile.

A smile that disappeared in a nanosecond.

"Daniel!" she cried, pointing into the distance. "Behind you!"

Chapter 68

I WHIPPED AROUND.

The earth shook.

A giant monster, a hideous beast at least 150 feet tall, was marching across the flat Kansas plains, heading straight for the farmhouse.

Number 1 was back. And it was definitely bigger and badder than ever, too. Its splayed feet, which were the size of a train car, looked like they belonged on a colossal three-toed raptor. Its body was all bumpy bone and slimy, gelatinous muscle, with no flesh to cover up all the rippling tendons and gristle. It had the curled, stinging tail of a scorpion, the serrated claws of a lobster, and the carbuncle-covered spine of a hunchback demon. As the nightmarish giant lurched forward, its lobster-claw hands dragged across the open fields, slicing deep furrows in the black soil.

But its head was the most hideous part of all.

It was nothing but an exposed brain made up of swirled, spongy globs of purple goo and pus-dripping boils. Some sort of gaseous cloud wavered in the air just above the rear of its curdled brain blob. Every now and then, the gas would erupt into bursts of blue flame.

Up front, burrowed into the brow of the jiggly mound of gray matter, were two hollow goggle holes instead of eyeballs. The thing had no snout, just a gas mask–shaped mouth hole filled with a pair of fleshy, flickering tongues— each one at least twenty feet long and tipped with a deadly stinger.

"What *is* that thing?" said Joe, who had quickly morphed his meatball sandwich into a supercharged laser-burst bazooka.

"Number 1," I said, sizing up the situation and running through all the new defensive strategies and classic battle strategies recently downloaded into my brain.

"I thought Number 1 was a big bug," said Emma. "A praying mantis."

"That was just the form it took. Until now..."

"Well," said Willy, "this new model is even uglier. Daniel? Joe? Can one of you guys materialize me a weapon and a ton of ammo?"

We both did. Simultaneously.

"Thanks," said Willy, balancing and leveling the two blasters. "I have a clean shot at those two frontal blow holes that might be its eyes."

"Impossible," said Joe. "The thing has to be two miles away."

Willy grinned. "Looks like *I* came back with laser guided vision."

"Cool."

The brain-headed beast kept pounding across the prairie on its skeletal stilts, tearing down power lines with its bony shins, flaring fireballs out of the back of its wet and wormy brain head.

"We should surround it," suggested Mel. "Have Willy aim for the knee joints. Its limbs are so spindly, if Willy knee-caps it, the whole teetering scaffold of bones will just topple to the ground."

"I like it," I said, glad to have my best friends since forever in the battle with me once again

"And I like our odds," said Willy. "The five of us against one Bony Moronie monster with a bad case of brain acne? Piece of cake."

And right about then is when a dark, undulating line appeared on the horizon.

The giant beast raised one of its arms high in the air like a Roman centurion.

"Charge!" it growled.

The line at the horizon swarmed forward. The new Number 1 had brought its legions with it. Millions and millions and millions of its dark followers carpeted the Kansas plains as far as my eyes could see.

And the whole stampeding horde was gunning straight for me and my friends.

Chapter 69

"OKAY," SAID WILLY. "The odds have changed. Slightly. But, hey—I still think we have a shot at winning this thing."

"Um, not to sound pessimistic," said Joe, "but when was the last time five teenagers beat a million evil minions led by a Godzilla-sized exoskeletal creep with a scorpion tail and lobster-claw hands?"

"The last time doesn't matter," I said. "All that counts is *this* time. We don't back down."

"No retreat," said Willy.

"No surrender," added Joe.

We all charged up our weapons.

"Aim for the brain," I said.

"Roger that," said Willy,

"Wait, you guys," said Emma, pointing at something behind us. "It looks like the cavalry just arrived."

We all spun around. There was a golden line on the opposite horizon.

A million and more warriors—many riding horses, elephants, and camels; all bathed in the warm glow of a massive sunbeam that followed their every move—came charging across the prairie. Trumpets and bugles blared.

Suddenly we had legions, too!

In the lead was a brilliant white steed ridden by a helmetless warrior in shimmering golden armor. Her wildly curled, dazzling hair swirled in the breeze as she galloped across the open fields like Joan of Arc with two glowing swords crossed above her head.

"It's Xanthos!" shouted Mel.

"And Mikaela!" I added.

"Who's she?"

"A friend of my father's."

Could this be the backup my dad had urged me to find? I wondered.

It sure looked and felt like it. Just like that, we were evenly matched. The Legions of the Light galloping past us were as numerous as the forces of darkness swarming across the open plains to do battle for Evil.

As Xanthos and Mikaela led the cavalry charge, my spiritual advisor's jolly voice reached out to my mind once more: *Remember, Daniel: You cannot fight hate with hate. You cannot eliminate darkness with something darker still. You can only destroy the evil with goodness and light.*

Millions of golden warriors, all armed with shining swords, streamed past us to do just that.

In an instant, they collided with Zeboul's massive army of disgustingly scuzzy creatures.

The battle was joined.

At stake was the future of Earth.

Maybe the entire universe.

Chapter 70

A SEVEN-DAY BATTLE commenced.

The fight raged on, day and night, for a full week.

We would send in a battalion of golden warriors armed with shimmering broadswords. Zeboul would counter with a brigade of skittering black creatures carrying three-pronged tridents.

Warrior after warrior evaporated into eternity.

Zeboul stayed back, beyond the fray. When we materialized guided missiles to take the monster down, it countered with anti-missile missiles.

The rockets, like our soldiers, canceled each other out, leaving the air above the battlefield thick with clouds of black and white smoke that mingled together to become dull and ominous gray thunderheads.

"This will never end," said Mel.

"There's no tipping point," added Emma. "Good and evil remain in constant balance. A surge on one side is countered by a surge on the other."

"It's a lose-lose situation," said Joe.

"But we can't give up!" urged Willy. "The battle between good and evil may never end, but it's still worth fighting!"

"Willy's right," I said. "In fact, it's the *only* battle worth fighting."

And so it went.

On the fifth day, Zeboul's mind reached out to mine to mock me.

"Remember what your mommy told you, Danny Boy? You are not immortal. You were foolish to return to this realm. At the end of every day, darkness always vanquishes the light."

"Until the light returns the next morning," I taunted back. "You can't win. Not here. Not on any planet where good creatures stand up and refuse to let you rule over them."

"Your soul is in grave danger, Danny Boy. If you die again, it will be as if your spirit never existed."

"You're the bigger fool," I shot back. "Every time you try to kill me, you just make me stronger. Strong enough to fix that black hole you poked through the Milky Way."

"Ha! You will never be strong enough to counter my creative destruction."

"Just watch me!"

But I couldn't just zoom off to do a quick black-hole repair job. Not while the battle dragged on.

I was needed to counter any move or sneak attack Zeboul's bloated brain cooked up.

Meanwhile, Mikaela was our field commander; Xanthos the bravest of our extremely brave warriors.

Wave after wave of legionnaires entered the fray. All of them disappeared, taking an equal number of enemy combatants off the board with them.

Light pierced shadow.

Shadow covered light.

On the seventh day, Mikaela herself vaporized as she took down Zeboul's top general.

"Mikaela!" became the battle cry of Xanthos and our few remaining troops.

My trusted advisor led our final charge.

He and our warriors raced at full speed into the last line still standing for the forces of darkness. Our last surviving soldiers erased their last surviving soldiers. Both sides melted into a mist and instantly disappeared.

The plains of Kansas were smoldering and black for miles in every direction. My old farmhouse was, once again, a heap of charred rubble.

"It's just us," said Willy.

My four friends were still at my side.

I stepped forward and laid down my weapon.

"No," I said. "This time, it's just me."

Chapter 71

"NO, DANIEL."

Mel grabbed me by the arm.

"I have to do this," I said. "If I fail, if I fall ... promise me you guys will take over for me and keep Terra Firma safe."

Willy nodded. Joe and Emma, too. Finally, Mel let go of my arm.

"Be careful," she whispered. "I think I'm only allowed one soul mate. So don't go and do anything stupid."

"I'll try."

Willy powered up his blaster. "Just in case that creep has a sniper hidden somewhere because it's too chicken to go mano a mano with you."

"I think it *is* part chicken," cracked Joe. "Have you seen that thing's feet? Bock-bock-BOCK."

As always, Joe made me smile.

"Daniel?" said Emma.

Usually, before any kind of combat she's the one who

urges me to show mercy on my opponent, no matter how foul or monstrous the creature might be.

Today, not so much.

"Take that ugly sucker down!"

"I'll do my best," I said. "Hang here, you guys. When I'm done with Zeboul, we have a black hole in the middle of the Milky Way to patch up or else we'll be goners in a couple of weeks, anyway."

I marched across the empty, scorched earth.

After a seven-day battle, there were no mountains of corpses or wounded warriors to be carted off the field. The millions of combatants on both sides who had bravely or blindly given up their life forces in this final showdown had all evaporated into nothingness.

As if they were never even here.

I figured this was the fate that awaited me if I couldn't find some way to eliminate Zeboul. Some way to overwhelm its staggering size and strength. At least, if I were vaporized when I took out Zeboul, my friends—fully loaded with their newfound powers—would live on after me to do the job I had been sent here to do: protect Earth from whatever new evil came its way.

The ground under my feet trembled.

I looked up to see Zeboul marching forward on its ginormous, bony legs. Its lobster claws were snapping open and shut like crazed, jumbo-sized crocodiles. The thing was so big it blocked out the sun and cast a cold shadow across my entire body.

I remembered the story of David and Goliath and thought about materializing a slingshot.

Because, for what had to be our final confrontation, Number 1 had turned itself into an indestructible, earth-shaking giant.

I, on the other hand, looked human. And small.

I was a tiny teenager going up against a colossal incarnation of the enemy that had plagued the universe since the dawn of creation.

I was a kid. It was a mammoth monster.

But, like Joe said, at least I didn't have big, honking chicken feet.

I narrowed my eyes and peered up at the 150-foot-tall monster.

"To destroy me, boy," the horrid creature bellowed, "you must be willing to obliterate yourself. To be vaporized like all your foolish foot soldiers and my mindless minions. Are you ready to end your existence, Daniel X?"

I nodded slowly. "If that's what it takes to end yours—Shorty!"

I could tell that calling IT "Shorty" puzzled the beast. It furrowed the brain ridges around its eye sockets.

Until, in a flash, I rearranged my molecules and imagined myself as huge as Zeboul. Then I tacked on ten extra feet so the slobbering giant would have to look up at me.

"Bring it on, pipsqueak," I cried out in a voice so big, it made those tongue things dangling out Zeboul's mouth hole flutter like wet towels in a wind tunnel.

"PREPARE TO DISAPPEAR, DANIEL!" it screamed.

"Only if you disappear first!" I hollered back.

Then both of its clasping claws shot up from the sides, aiming for a huge and easy target: my newly gigantic neck.

Chapter 72

I DUCKED DOWN into a squat the instant the double pincers were half a foot from my throat.

Zeboul screamed in pain when his snappers found nothing to bite into but each other. I tucked and rolled, crushing a couple of torched apple trees in the process.

Yeah, when titans tangle, there's going to be all sorts of collateral damage on the ground. In a way, it was good that the seven-day battle had left these Kansas plains a barren wasteland of shriveled and charred debris. Otherwise, we would have knocked it all down with our wrestling moves.

I remembered what Mel had said about the giant beast's knees being its weak spot. They were nothing but a clanking collection of meatless bones. If I kicked it in its knobby knees I was certain the whole skeleton would come crashing down.

So I morphed my sneakers into steel-toed work boots, leaped up, and sent out a roundhouse kick straight at the gangly creature's brittle legs.

Half a second before steel met kneecap, Zeboul clamped my ankle in the vise grip of a lobster claw.

Then it swung me around and around like I was a shot-put and he was on the Giants' Olympics Team, and hurled me up into the sky.

I was thrown halfway up to Alpar Nok and back. I came crashing back to Earth, traveling at twice the speed of light. So when I reentered the atmosphere and made impact with the hard Kansas prairie ground, my mind went blank.

I was so stunned, I let the big beast stomp on my head with its hook-toed raptor feet. Pumping its leg like a pile driver, Zeboul pummeled me a couple of miles down into the ground. Then, quickly extending the length of its bony arms, it reached down into my silo-sized wormhole and plucked me out.

It held me up in front of those hollow eyeholes and flicked its double tongues in and out of its slimy, sideways-opening mandibles.

I remembered the scorpion stingers at the tip of its tongues.

"Prepare for nothingness, Daniel. Now I will send you into the black void of nonexistence."

Double stingers poked up out of the tongues.

I tried to imagine myself free from the beast's grip.

I tried to imagine that I was the size of a tick.

I tried to imagine I had an Opus 24/24 aimed at its head.

But its mind read my mind and countered every one of my desperate ideas.

It was hopeless. This thing was too powerful.

There was absolutely no way for me to single-handedly defeat the raw, negative energy of pure unbridled evil.

My soul was about to be obliterated.

Chapter 73

SUDDENLY I HEARD the loudest voice anyone has ever heard anywhere on the earth.

It was louder than thunder echoing across the Grand Canyon.

Louder than the explosion of the volcano that buried Pompeii.

"You must have a backup, Daniel! ALWAYS!"

Chapter 74

STARTLED, ZEBOUL DROPPED me and turned to face the voice. I couldn't believe what I saw.

My father.

Only he was 170 feet tall.

I heard the crunch of bones. Zeboul was making itself taller. Matching my father, inch for inch.

"*YOU!*" it screamed as it grew. "You are not allowed to return to this realm!"

"I know," said my father. "But I did it anyway."

"You will lose your immortal soul!"

"Only after you lose yours! You should never have come after my son!"

My father started running straight for Number 1, the same way the Legions of the Light went charging at the forces of darkness. He had to be moving 500 miles per hour. Number 1 was matching him, stride for stride. They were two blurs: atomic-powered freight trains racing toward a head-on collision.

"No, Dad!" I screamed. I couldn't take losing him again. "Don't!"

But he kept charging.

So did Number 1.

The two of them made impact.

The whole world shuddered and quaked and went blindingly white in a burst of blistering light.

I heard my father's final triumphant words: "I love you, Daniel. *Always.*"

And then there was nothing but a cloud of sparkling dust drifting down in a collapsing silhouette of the enormous space the two giant warriors once occupied.

They had both imploded into oblivion.

The sparkling remnants of their earthly existence weren't gold or violet. They were flawlessly clear, icy crystals of nothingness. A gusty wind swirled across the plains and they were both gone.

Forever.

The ultimate good and the ultimate evil had canceled each other out.

Because my father, the best man I have ever known, had come back. He had sacrificed his own afterlife of happiness to avenge what happened here all those years ago.

He came back to Kansas and took down his own killer.

He protected Terra Firma.

He saved me.

My father was, and always had been, my very best backup.

Chapter 75

MY FATHER WAS gone.

He had given up his very existence in this life and beyond. He would never return to my mother in the after-life again. Or to me.

I glanced over at my friends just to make sure they were still there. They were no longer one-hundred-percent purely products of my imagination. They were alive. They were living and breathing and staring in awe at the already fading memory of my father's final heroic battle.

Joe was laughing. Willy was whooping wildly and pumping his fist in the air. Mel and Emma were both shedding tears for my loss.

Emotions were definitely running high because, like I was saying, they were all very much alive again.

I couldn't explain how all this happened, what power in the universe was ultimately responsible.

I just had to accept it.

And so I did. With a ton of humility and gratitude.

"Thanks, Dad," I whispered to the wind. "Thanks for everything."

And then I looked up to the heavens and echoed his famous last words: "I love you. Always."

EPILOGUE

Chapter 76

I'M STILL NOT one-hundred-percent certain if I returned to life with new powers like my four friends did.

I do know that all the powers I currently possess received some kind of tremendous booster shot. My imagination had been so intensely magnified it was almost strong enough for me to single-handedly eliminate the gaping black hole Number 1 had punched through the fabric of the galaxy. But, like my dad always said, I needed backup.

He was also right about a backup being a strength, not a weakness. If you have backup, you'll never be alone. Hey, I've been there. Done the all-alone thing. Letting someone cover your back and lend you a hand is way better.

So, with a little help from my four incredibly awesome friends, including Mel's recently discovered ability to manipulate the space-time continuum, we got 'er done. That's why, when you look up in the night sky, you don't notice anything out of whack. All the stars are back in their proper positions.

After eliminating Zeboul's final threat to Terra Firma, Mel, Emma, Willy, Joe, and I returned to Kansas.

This time we didn't rebuild my childhood home. Instead, we threw together the most awesome crib any teenager could imagine. There were more game rooms than bedrooms and all the walls had at least two flat-screen TVs. The freezer in the basement was stocked with Ben & Jerry's (every flavor), White Castle sliders, and jumbo cases of Hot Pockets. The kitchen had five microwaves: no waiting.

There was also a self-regenerating nacho bar. That was Joe's idea.

That night we threw the biggest victory party the world has probably ever seen.

Not that there would ever be a final victory for any of us against the forces of evil. I knew that I hadn't defeated IT forever. Somehow, darkness would always find a way to seep back into life to challenge the light. But, for the moment, evil was in full retreat. For now, good had emerged triumphant.

And that was reason enough to party.

Joe took care of all the eats. He brought in this famous chef named Wolfgang Puck to make everybody gourmet California-style pizzas. Stuff like spicy Thai chicken pizza and pizza with smoked salmon and caviar. He also did a couple of pepperoni pies for Willy.

Emma took care of the vegetarian stuff. Including a whole truckload of vegan cakes, cookies, and pies.

"Hey," she said, "it's a party!"

Mel did the decorations—including balloons. As in hot-air balloons you could take for a ride across the open prairie (which, by the way, the five of us imagined back to its full amber-waves-of-grain beauty).

Willy was in charge of games. To help out, I summoned up several Olympic sprinters for the potato sack races.

I also materialized Rihanna and Pharrell to assume DJ responsibilities. And, I invited (and transported) a bunch of friends from our past adventures. Chordata the elephant was there and let everybody ride on her back. Merlin the magician showed up and did a couple of really awesome tricks with Criss Angel. A bunch of the kids from this one high school I had gone to (for like two minutes) came and had an amazing time.

Agent Judge was there, too. So was my friend, the Navy SEAL.

We even invited Pork Chop. She had a blast dancing with One Direction. What can I say? She's young. She's Pork Chop.

All and all it was, without a doubt, The Party of the Century.

I wished, of course, that my mother and father could've been there to savor our victory, no matter how temporary it might prove to be.

Speaking of my dad, I just pray that if I ever have a son, I never forget the lesson he taught me: Being a father means being willing to sacrifice everything for the sake of your children.

Everything.

"Are you going to pick a new last name?" asked Mel as we sat together at the edges of the party, watching Pharrell rocking out with Beethoven on piano (I told you it was the party of the century, maybe the millennium).

I frowned. "What's wrong with 'X'? I think it's awesome."

She giggled. "It's easy to spell, so that's a plus." All of a sudden, she looked serious. "So what's next, Daniel?"

I just sort of shrugged. "I'm not sure."

"So is this it? No more outlaws to hunt, no more worlds to save? The Alien Hunter is officially going into retirement?"

"For now." I knew I was being vague, but my future *was* vague. Even though I'd achieved what I had dedicated my whole life to do, I hadn't quite accepted that my purpose was fulfilled. "What do I know about fate and the universe and how it all works? I'm just a teenager. Learning stuff is what we do."

Mel smirked. "You're not *just* a teenager. But if learning is what you need, I'm willing to teach you a few things."

I raised an eyebrow. "Like what?"

"Well..." She looked out at the exuberant scene before us, with our friends looking as if they were having the most fun ever. Then she turned back to me, the lights reflected in her eyes. "Like how to be happy."

I felt a lump form in my throat as her words sank in. As an outsider whose parents were ripped away when I needed them most, and whose childhood has been spent hunting and hiding from the worst killers in the universe,

I thought of *happiness* as a wisp of smoke that never failed to vanish after a few moments.

Things were going to be different from here on out, I knew. But now that there were no aliens left to hunt, would I be happy as a "normal" kid? With real, non-imaginary friends and school and a job and...a girlfriend?

I had no idea where my life was going to lead, but I did know one thing—whatever happened, I wouldn't ever be alone again. My backup would be there for me. *Always*.

Mel was looking at me expectantly. I stood up and pulled her next to me. Hands locked, we started for our friends, who were laughing so hard they could hardly stand.

Would I be happy as a normal kid?

I couldn't wait to find out.

About the Author

James Patterson has had more #1 bestsellers for children than any other living writer. He is the author of the Middle School, I Funny, Treasure Hunters, and Daniel X novels, as well as *House of Robots*. His blockbuster fiction for adults, featuring enduring characters like Alex Cross—in addition to his many books for teens, such as the Maximum Ride series—have sold more than 300 million copies worldwide. He lives in Florida.

Chris Grabenstein is a *New York Times* bestselling author who has also collaborated with James Patterson on the I Funny and Treasure Hunters series and *House of Robots*. He lives in New York City.